HEATHER S. CHAUVIN

Camp Sunshine

A Thrilling Domestic Novella

Library of Congress Control Number: 2024925381

Book Cover by Getcovers.

First edition

ISBN: 979-8-9911409-1-1

This book was professionally typeset on Reedsy.
Find out more at reedsy.com

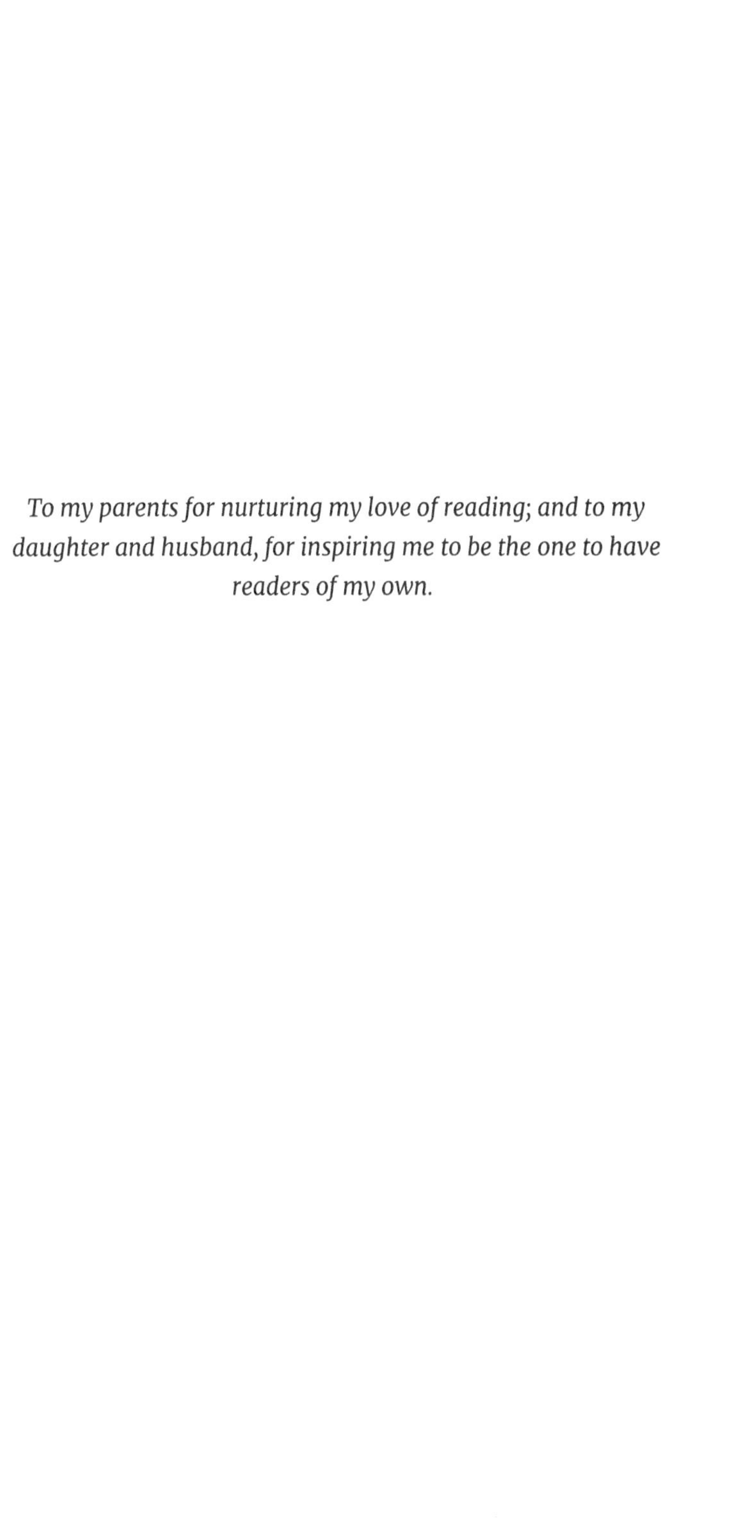

To my parents for nurturing my love of reading; and to my daughter and husband, for inspiring me to be the one to have readers of my own.

For man is not the only creature that
hunts for sport, it is the only creature
capable of not having to hunt at all.

— Devin Schieffler

Contents

Prologue   1

I   Part One

Chapter One   5
    Brooke   5
Chapter Two   10
    Brooke   10
Chapter Three   20
    Brooke   20
Chapter Four   26
    Brooke   26
Chapter Five   34
    Brooke   34
Chapter Six   38
    Brooke   38
Chapter Seven   43
    Brooke   43
Chapter Eight   47
    Brooke   47
Chapter Nine   50
    CJ   50
Chapter Ten   56
    Brooke   56

Chapter Eleven 61
Brooke 61
Chapter Twelve 67
Brooke 67
Chapter Thirteen 71
Brooke 71
Chapter Fourteen 75
Brooke 75
Chapter Fifteen 80
Brooke 80
Chapter Sixteen 85
Brooke 85
Chapter Seventeen 90
Brooke 90
Chapter Eighteen 98
Brooke 98
Chapter Nineteen 102
Brooke 102
Chapter Twenty 107
Brooke 107

II   Part Two

Chapter Twenty-One 115
CJ 115
Chapter Twenty-Two 121
CJ 121
Chapter Twenty-Three 124
CJ 124
Chapter Twenty-Four 129
CJ 129

Chapter Twenty-Five   134
    CJ   134

III   Part Three

Chapter Twenty-Six   139
    Brooke   139
Chapter Twenty-Seven   143
    Brooke   143
Chapter Twenty-Eight   148
    Brooke   148
Chapter Twenty-Nine   154
    Brooke   154
Chapter Thirty   158
    Brooke   158
Chapter Thirty-One   161
    Dr. G   161

Epilogue   166
    Brooke   166
Acknowledgments   168
About the Author   170

Prologue

I force my eyes open, pushing against the fear that dirt will fall into them, but all I see is complete darkness. And all I feel is a strong sense of foreboding. This is easily the most terrified I have ever been.

I search my memories for an explanation, some way to explain how I got into this situation, but my thoughts are cloudy and jumbled. I'm trying—I really am—but I can't remember exactly how I wound up here. It's as if I'm walking through a void. There are no photos, no shelves, nothing except fog billowing at my feet and up into emptiness.

Hesitantly, I glance around, and as I do, a sharp pain radiates through my neck. I wince and wait for the wave of pain to pass before trying to reach up and explore the boundaries of my prison. But as I lift my arm, expecting it to glide through open air, I learn that I am unable to move. My advance is restricted by something soft that holds firm against the back of my hand. I flip my hand over slowly to analyze the material with the pads of my fingertips. The fabric itself is soft and thin, but something semisolid presses against the opposite side. Small, almost-indiscernible specks filter through the thin sheet. Dirt.

It's then that I feel the heat of my exhalations, bouncing back onto my face. I attempt to calm myself, taking small breaths, unsure of how much longer I'll have access to oxygen.

I try again to lift my heavy arm to the side and again find

myself halted by the fabric. I try to pull my arms back and push myself up to a seated position, but I realize that I'm too weak. The gravity of a forceful and heavy weight rests atop my body, immobilizing me further. Even just trying to lift my head takes significant effort, and I give up, my head falling back an inch, down onto solid ground, unforgiving under my weight.

This black abyss, paired with my inability to move... I'm going to die here.

I'm not only buried in my own body but buried in the ground. It isn't solely my thoughts that are foggy, but my ability to move is impaired and restricted as well.

I never imagined I'd be buried alive. Well, perhaps I've had an intrusive thought, but never to be taken seriously. How does something like this even happen to someone like me? I don't go to the shady spots around town. I try to always be on the lookout for predators in the grocery store. I try not to trust strangers, and I mean *try* because I'm a people pleaser and sometimes I fall victim to smooth talkers. *Okay, Brooke, focus. Where am I?*

I stare into the unnerving darkness before slamming my eyes shut in defeat. I dig into the recesses of my mind, attempting to recall how I ended up here. Snapshots begin to appear suddenly before quickly dissolving, transitioning rapidly into a frightening tale. Scenes, both assaulting and ambivalent, come back to me in a fleeting succession before disappearing, replaced by the realization of what happened. Now I realize that I am truly on the verge of death, and I deserve it.

I

Part One

Chapter One

Brooke

Then

Yes, it's finally time.

Now we can officially begin our long weekend away with family and friends. As I look out the windshield, I see that we have arrived at the campground, and immediately, I am amazed at the views here in rural Mississippi. We turn down a hidden lane, off the highway, and embark down a serpentine trail lined with nothing but red dirt, overgrown shrubbery, and rows upon rows of billowing pine trees. It's not that I haven't observed scenery like this before, but I hadn't anticipated coming across it a mere two hours from home. The landscape of Louisiana is significantly different from what I perceive in front of me.

Back at home, all we have is flat land as far as one can see, with not a dip nor hill for miles—not to mention water in the form of bayous, ditches, lakes, or ponds, typically within feet of the roadside.

I've always felt an ethereal connection to creeks and the wilderness, but until this moment, I assumed that I had to travel as far as Tennessee to be rewarded with the kind of view I now find in front of me.

"Wow, this place is beautiful," I utter, as if I lack the vocabulary to fully verbalize my feelings.

I don't attempt to modify my previous utterance. My statement will have to suffice. My neighbor, who is sitting in the driver's seat next to me, looks my way.

"Yes, why do you think we love to come here?" she asks.

I laugh because I wasn't expecting much. I simply assumed they came for the cheap price of the camper rental spots.

I hardly ever go camping anymore. Actually, it has been almost twenty years since I've been, and even then I was only a child. Now, at age twenty-nine, I'm faced with a completely different experience.

When I was young, I jumped into the family van, accompanied by my parents, grandparents, and cousins, pulling a travel trailer. This time around, it's me, my husband, and my eighteen-month-old daughter joining our neighbors and their daughter, who is only slightly older than ours. Our husbands drive ahead of us, pulling the camper and golf cart trailer, while we trail behind with the children, groceries, and luggage. Later today, a pair of our neighbors' close friends will be here, too, and they'll join us on what is sure to be a camping adventure.

This experience is going to be different from those that I've had in the past because I'm no longer just along for the ride. I don't get to tag along and have carefree fun like I did as a child. I'm responsible for taking care of another human life as well as for organizing, cleaning, and being a hospitable, caring, and neighborly friend.

Nonetheless, I am excited to enjoy a few days off from work, where I provide therapy services to children as an occupational therapist. I truly am looking forward to spending time in the dense, quiet woods with two children instead of encountering the usual dozen or so kids I interact with each day at work.

I wouldn't do my job if it wasn't something I'm passionate about. But picking up after and reprimanding so many kids gets to be a lot when you do it every weekday and then still have to come home and clean up after your own child and—it goes without mentioning—your husband too.

Suddenly, the taillights glow red ahead of us, indicating that our husbands are coming to a halt, and we come to a stop behind them. It appears that after searching and winding our way through the campground, they have finally located our assigned campsite. They're sure to begin the process of preparing the camper to serve as our temporary home for the next three days. The first thing they do upon exiting the vehicle is begin to unload the golf cart from the attached trailer so they can back the camper into our designated spot.

How delightful it would be to go for a ride and observe our surroundings while the men do all the hard work. After all, we have the girls, and we can't be expected to let them run around on such a busy day when there are active motorists, as other campers will be arriving today as well. Or at least that's the excuse I concoct in an attempt to try to worm out of the manual labor of getting settled.

Julia and I remain in the car as we wait for our husbands to navigate and secure the camper to our designated site. I imagine this entails connecting the electricity, sewage, and plumbing. I'm lucky enough not to know myself how to do those things, and therefore, I am able to avoid being assigned those duties, at least.

A shuffling sound begins from behind me, and with that,

I surmise that the girls must be starting to stir awake in the back seat. Fortunately, they are still young, so any car ride of more than an hour is easy to get away with as the soft bouncing motion soothes them to sleep. As they begin to raise the volume of their babbling, Julia and I share a glance and a shrug as we decide that the men have gotten enough of the work done. We can now proceed with preparing the inside of the camper.

We both exit her SUV after she parks, and I pause a moment to take in the nearby scenery. It really is a nice spot, not so near the lake's edge that I have to worry about my daughter wandering off but close enough that we have a beautiful view of the water. There's a generous distance between our site and the one next to us, which offers us an enhanced notion of privacy. Although we just exited the vehicle, the heat rushes over me. I'm sure if we linger outside for more than five minutes, I'll feel the sweat begin to bead down my back.

Kent, my husband, speaks, and I focus my attention on him.

"We're going to find a boulder to stabilize the back of the camper," he announces.

Julia perks up and says, "In that case, we will wait for y'all to get back to begin our device detox."

I groan internally as I recall the agreement that was made among us all—to ditch our devices for the weekend in an attempt to make more memories and enjoy each other's company.

As our husbands drive off in the golf cart, I think about how it's not that I don't agree with the idea of a detox, but it's that I don't think the absence of our devices will increase social interaction among everyone.

When these guys get together, phones or not, they huddle up and seek adventure, always leaving the women to take care of the children and pets. We don't have to worry about the dogs this weekend, at least, as they've stayed behind with family. Four Labradors and an Australian shepherd are a bit much for a four-bed camper that is already crowded with six adults and two children.

Outside and surrounded by nature, I have been eagerly awaiting the opportunity to spend time with my husband, our neighbors, their friends, and our girls. I won't get my hopes up, though, because the best way to not be disappointed is to not expect much at all in the first place. I slacken my shoulders and mentally prepare for the weekend as I make my way to the back passenger door to unbuckle my daughter from her car seat.

Chapter Two

Brooke

Then

I finish taking my daughter, Erin, out of her car seat and place her on the ground. As I direct her away from the road, I pull my phone from my pocket and try to open one of my apps in anticipation of losing access to my social media. I check it quickly, as I don't want to take my eyes off Erin for too long, and I notice that I barely have one bar of service at all. I try to refresh the feed, and I'm unsuccessful in prompting new content to appear. Laughing at myself, I slip it back into my pocket because even if I could use my phone this weekend, I wouldn't technically have any service to do anything with it. I watch Erin sit down and begin to play in the dirt. I smile, happy to know that she isn't afraid to make a mess. Julia's daughter, Rachel, is walking aimlessly nearby. I can't help but feel like she is testing the boundaries and seeing how far she can get without being intercepted. Although she is only two, she is fierce and full of spirit.

Much like their mothers are to one another, our girls are like fire and ice, so opposite in their mannerisms and personalities. Rachel is adventurous, confrontational, and particularly fearless for her age until she encounters something that she can't comprehend. When faced with sharp edges and steep cliffs, she charges without a thought. But when it comes to giant slides spewing substantial amounts of water and oversized animals in festive attire, she rightfully clings to her mother in terror.

Meanwhile, Erin is curious, whimsical, and hesitant to participate in unfamiliar activities. Initially, upon finding the aforementioned steep cliff, Erin would likely shy away and analyze her predicament. She'd attempt to explore, hurt herself, or encounter some kind of discomfort, which would then lead her to find an escape, aka the alcove of my legs.

Rachel's personality is as much like her mother's as Erin's is to mine. I like to say my daughter gets a majority of her looks, intelligence, and personality from her dad, but it isn't completely true. Not that I don't have ideal characteristics. It's just that I admire her father's courage and superficial traits more so than my own. Erin is speculative and cautious like me, and I become more aware of this the older she gets. I can candidly identify my flaws just as easily as I can point out my redeeming qualities. For example, while I am educated, having acquired dual college degrees and excelling in academia with an A grade point average, occasionally I lack common sense and the ability to connect the dots.

Just as Rachel and Erin are so different, the same can be said for Julia and me. It really is remarkable how two people who can appear so different can get along so well. From the moment that we noticed we had new neighbors, Kent and I would discuss so many possibilities and hypothetical interactions with them.

We'd speculate about who they could be. Would they have

kids? Be just like us? Be rich and take us on their yacht? Aggravate us? Attempt to convince us to be swingers? Be rude? Have substantial emotional baggage? There were so many possibilities, and we knew nothing about them.

Then one night when Kent and I were out at the local bar across the bayou, we bumped into them. We apologized profusely for being lousy neighbors and not introducing ourselves and sought forgiveness for the absence of baked goods, which is mostly attributed to the fact that I am not the baking type. They apologized in return for not walking over themselves.

After that, we all hung out together and had a great night. The music was so loud that it sounded distorted through the speakers, and Julia and I danced carelessly through the night, amid the aura of our small town and its unassuming people. Our husbands lingered at a high-top table, formulating conversations about boats, work, and the entertainment that one can enjoy on all-terrain vehicles. That was the night that we established our friendship, and although I quickly identified that we had differences, overall we got along well.

So much so that shortly after meeting, we became so close that when Julia announced she was pregnant with her first child, I consequently informed my husband that we had to be next. Luckily, my husband agreed, and our daughters were born six months apart.

Initially, when we were getting to know one another, I had not pegged Julia to be someone I'd get along with so well. Whereas I am shy and timid, she is ostentatious and lively. While I like to sit in the back of a room unnoticed, she likes to stand at the front with all eyes on her. I can't imagine a world where my personality would ever be reflective of hers. It's almost alien to me that she can be so confident and verbal about her needs to all who will listen, while I feel like I'm never heard at all. It seems that the best friendships are made that way, not by having endless similarities but by allowing differences to impact one another. We have a companionship in the sense that she can be a part of me that I am unable to portray, while I provide the same for her.

The thing I like about Julia is that we're not best friends, but we don't have to be in order to connect. I enjoy that we can debate, both with valid concerns and points, and that we have opportunities for discussion and to educate one another instead of agreeing and/or fighting. I learn so much more in life that way—by being open-minded to opinions. I don't like to rock the boat anyway, and I prefer as little confrontation as possible.

I am able to observe my timidness reflected in my child as Rachel bulldozes through Erin, pushing her onto the ground and into a cloud of red dust. Erin shrieks with fear and looks at me as if to ask me to defend her. I blush and glance toward Julia before rushing to my child, sweeping her up into my arms to console her. I hear Julia reprimand Rachel behind me, which is appropriate since I surely don't have the audacity to do so.

"Are you all caught up on that show I recommended?" she asks me.

Julia and I carry on and spend time chatting, and even though we talked the whole hour and a half here, we continue to find topics to gab about.

Eventually, Julia says, "Guess we can go inside."

It's beginning to get dark, so Erin and I follow Julia toward the camper to escape the soon-to-be onslaught of mosquitoes. We look at each other as we approach the stairs.

"Time for a challenge! Ready to get everything settled in there?" I ask Julia.

"True," she replies in a mocking tone. "We have to get things where they belong and prepare a meal, all while simultaneously attempting to corral the children so we can maintain order."

"Looks like it's all on us to watch the kids and get everything done in here."

We both smile and roll our eyes because we realize that this isn't much different from what we each do within our respective homes. Just as, I'm sure, many housewives do, have done, and will continue to do long after we are gone.

Julia and I consistently have the most fluent conversations about spousal responsibilities—or lack thereof. It's one of our most tenacious subjects.

I raise my eyebrows and sarcastically say, "Come on, Julia, let's pawn the kids off on someone else because it's impossible to get anything done when we have to watch them."

"That's exactly what Jacob would do if he were me. He'd ask his aunt to come pick Rachel up. Funny how I can always get things done with her, but he can't."

"Watch and be amazed, boys," I say as I follow Julia into the camper.

The stairs lead up to a very small dining area, indicated by the tiny table that sits across from the door. On the right, up a short step, is the bathroom and the master bedroom. On the left is a small kitchen, and across the room, next to the table, sits a sofa. Beyond the living area, there is the back bedroom, which holds one set of bunk beds. I take a left and walk toward what will serve as our bedroom for the weekend.

It just so happens that our room is also storage for all the objects that don't have a true home. Essentially, our room serves as a temporary resting place for all the stuff that is usually left outside or the things that may fall during transit.

In order to have somewhere to sleep tonight, I absolutely have to rehome all the things that were squirreled away in there.

Before I begin to bring things outside, I check on the girls and find them playing in the main bedroom. I slowly walk myself backward, trying not to disturb their concentration as well as ensuring that they won't get between my feet while I move stuff around.

I carry outside the folding chairs as well as the outdoor burner, propane tank, and cornhole boards. As I'm bringing out the patio rug, the guys pull up with a boulder four times the size of my head and just as unevenly shaped, as I'm sure mine is underneath all my thin dirty-blond hair.

"You're using that to stabilize the camper?" I ask Kent in disbelief.

"No, the camper is already stable. This is going to make it even better."

I look at them skeptically as I walk back into the camper. Now that I've made some headway, I enter our room, take the pillow mattress from the top bunk, and place it on the futon below. I take all our bags off the bottom bunk and put them on the floor so that I can make our bed.

"Where do you keep the sheets?" I yell to Julia from across the length of the camper.

"They're in our room," she says as she ejects the slide-out portion of the camper. I walk across to the front of the camper and find the sheets at the foot of her already-made bed.

Both girls are still entertaining themselves with things around the camper, likely having pulled items off shelves, and haphazardly relocating the throw pillows from the sofa. I may never get over the fact that we do everything with children in tow.

I rush back to my end of the camper and struggle to fit the snug sheets onto the mattress and topper. Of course, the girls choose this moment to focus on my efforts and crawl on top just as I finish affixing the sheet. At least the bed is made, for the most part, so I'll let them linger and tend to the blankets later. No use in trying to make it perfect if the girls are going to be on top of it. I throw on a couple pillows and check off that task in my head.

As I walk out of our room, Julia comes in with the groceries from the car. Now it's time to put into the pantry all the food we brought and feed the girls supper. I let Julia do almost all the organizing since it's her camper, and I set to work making a sandwich for the girls to share. I try not to bother Julia much as I dig around and orient myself to where everything is.

"Plates are above the stove," she chimes as she sees me rummaging through cabinets.

I finally serve the girls each a half sandwich and some chips as I survey our work. It looks like I was dreading all of this for nothing. If that's the most work I have to do all weekend long, I'm lucky.

"Want some pasta?" Julia asks me, and I nod eagerly in response.

To my surprise, and to my dismay, she pulls a chilled pasta salad out of the fridge. She sees the disappointment register on my face.

"I'm trying to make healthier choices," she states defensively.

"As am I, technically." I laugh, grabbing the empty plastic bowl that she hands me.

The two of us fix our plates and sit at the table with the girls Erin paws at my fork as I dig in, and I share some with her as

Julia shares with Rachel.

The door to the camper suddenly swings open, and our husbands walk in.

"Ohhh, what's that?" Kent asks.

"Here, you can use mine," I say as I hand him my empty bowl.

I watch them each serve themselves generous portions before they come to sit down at the table. As they sit, Julia and I get up and take the girls from the table to clean their hands. We clean up the girls, exchange looks with one another, and almost simultaneously appear to have the same thought.

Julia is quicker than me, though, as she speaks first. "Before it gets too dark, should we take a tour of the campground?"

"You know it!" I blurt out eagerly, almost before she has a chance to finish her sentence.

A brief thought passes through my mind. We should leave the girls with their fathers so that Julia and I can have a vestige of peace on what is our weekend away, but I quickly deem the thought selfish.

Before Julia has the chance to recommend that Kent and Jacob watch the kids, I say, "All right, girls, who wants to go for a ride?"

Julia laughs, and she says, "Yeah, let's go make some wind."

I look at her, feeling my face twist in confusion, and repeat her phrase questioningly. "Make wind?"

She laughs again as she glances toward Jacob and says, "Yes! When it's hot and the air is stagnant, we get on the golf cart to go cool off. Especially since the last time we came, we forgot a fan, and trust me, it was sweltering!"

I nod in understanding. This is their camper, and camping is their thing. It seems that they've done this a few times, and they have expectations for the weekend. I'll trust her to lead because they've camped more often and more recently than we have.

This particular camping place is called Pleasant Valley Campground and is actually one of their favorite places to visit. They try to come at least once a year and claim it's due to the scenic wilderness that it offers, which I have yet to fully explore.

We look at our husbands with inviting eyes, but Jacob says, "Y'all go on ahead. We'll grub right quick and then finish setting up here."

I smile and nod, not surprised by their decision to stay behind. Even at home, the guys are quick to do handy household tasks outdoors rather than spend time with us and the kids. I can't help but find conflict in this, mostly because prior to the birth of our daughter, my husband always prioritized time with me. I occasionally speculate about why that has changed.

Is it because a kid is a job in itself? An unpleasant job, and that's why he now tends to withdraw from us? Or would he have acted like this regardless of whether we had children or not?

I often tell myself to shut out the negative thoughts and embrace the positives. For instance, at least he is doing useful projects around the house. I tell myself I'd rather he be home than out at the local bars. Whenever our husbands are off doing random things, Julia and I often call it fucking off, no matter what they're up to.

I am easy to convince, but Julia, not so much. In her defense, her husband may fuck off, but he does it to a greater extent than my husband. Jacob will often go out to the bars, as well as disappear for hours without telling her where he went. Many times he has returned home with no remorse but always with an excuse prepared for his inquisitive wife. He does it so often that he has started to recycle excuses, the most common one being, "I was helping an old pal with something that he couldn't handle on his own."

I know all of these things because Julia and I often commiserate over text while we glance at the clock. Any time it gets past eleven p.m., she is texting me, *Can you believe he isn't home?*

Typically, I sympathize with her and lend an ear as well as complain about my own husband's mistakes. Luckily for me, an overwhelming majority of the time, I don't have the same complaints that she does. For this, I am thankful, but I try not to gloat.

Instead, I'm ashamed to admit this, but I usually stoke the fire. I comment with phrases like "He knows how you feel about it, and he keeps doing it" and "Of course you have to work a full day and come home to take care of your child alone, while he has the entire day to do as he pleases."

I shouldn't, but I can't help myself. I get just as upset as Julia because, if he were my husband, I would be *livid*. But as much as she complains, she still went and made another baby with him, as Julia is expecting their second child.

She actually tried to leave him when Rachel was only a few months old. He begged her not to divorce him, and he convinced her into staying for the sake of their daughter. He grew up in a home with divorced parents, and he pleaded with her, asking her to reconsider and keep their family intact. She stayed with him so that her child would not have to grow up in a broken home.

We walk out of the camper and into a glistening evening, with the sun beginning to set among the darkening clouds. Julia and I are about to not only make memories with our girls but also make wind as we partake in our own version of fucking off.

Chapter Three

Brooke

Then

Julia hops onto the driver's seat of the golf cart, and I throw the girls next to her before lifting myself onto the passenger side. I glance down and double-check to make sure the girls fit snugly between us before I give Julia the glance to go ahead. Before she presses the foot pedal, I pause and ask, "Wait. Can you even ride in this thing while pregnant?"

"Well, I did the same thing when I was pregnant with Rachel, and she's fine," Julia responds, shrugging.

I guess I can't argue with that logic.

"The last thing that we need is to be going uphill when the battery dies," Julia says as she looks down at the meter that shows a full battery.

She flashes me her perfect smile, which is supposed to reassure me, and I quickly admire her silky light-brown hair, which is almost always held up in a claw clip.

Julia is just naturally beautiful, and any makeup only accentuates her flawless features. She has large amber-colored eyes that reflect the setting sun and freckles that span lightly over the bridge of her nose. She is also tall, with a healthy figure, which she can attribute to our newly acquired exercise journey.

Right after we met, and before we both got pregnant, we started exercising together. It started with short walks and some weight lifting, but as the girls grew, so did our fondness for physical activity. We have been consistently exercising together, and it has done wonders for our mental health and even more so for our physical health. Although she is four months pregnant, only her belly has grown, and even that is barely noticeable.

Julia presses the pedal, and the neon-yellow golf cart lurches forward, which makes me instinctually stick my arm out in order to protect the girls from hitting the dashboard.

As I retract my arm, I reflect on my appearance and look down in order to examine my muffin top. It is slightly discouraging to be so physically active for so long and to still not have my old body back, but I guess that's what happens when one creates and births another life-form. I don't have good eating habits, though, so I'm not technically giving it my all. My inadequate diet leaves me with consistent breakouts along my chin, and my straw-colored hair lacks shine, no matter what expensive hair product I use. I roll my eyes. There is no need to be so hard on myself. I recite my mantra, the one instilled in me by my mother—I am beautiful, and I am intelligent. It could be worse.

I continue to manifest these things as Julia haphazardly drives us through the campground. This must be an older campground, judging by the pebbled road and narrow lanes. She takes a shortcut and drives through an empty camper slot and onto what appears to be the main road. Thankfully, she comes to a halt at the upcoming intersection before taking a sharp right.

We haven't gone this way yet, and I turn my head from side to side, admiring the lush forestry that lines the road on either side.

As we drive through the wooded area, cars travel toward us in the opposite lane, but none lurk behind us. I can't help but hope that we're allowed to drive on this road and that we aren't breaking any rules. Just thinking about us being in the wrong sends a tinge of anxiety through me. I have always had an affinity for following the rules, as the fear of being caught instills me with so much apprehension.

We pass what appears to be an outdoor church as well as a dilapidated gazebo that appears to be suspiciously close to being condemned. We emerge from the woods onto the base of an expansive valley. To our left is a boat launch, which lies at the foot of a murky lake. My eyes follow the road that we're on farther ahead to see that it travels up a steep hill. I admire how it climbs before us and begins to curve around the lake, forming a cliff high above the water. At the foot of the hill, there appears to be another road on the left that leads into another valley into which the lake appears to narrow significantly and flow through.

Julia drives straight past the busy boat launch, and we make our way toward the foot of the hill. I imagine that we are going up the hill, based on her comment from earlier, but I can't help but speculate as to what we might find if we were to take the road winding around the base of the hill instead—a river, creek, waterfall, or a smaller pond possibly? As we continue our journey, my eyes shift to the right, and I appreciate the presence of the dense wooded area accompanied by a shallow stream of water, resembling a ditch, that flows alongside the tree line.

Just as I had suspected, we begin to make our ascent up the hill. I look at my daughter so that I may watch her expressions unfold, as we have never had an adventure together quite like this before. I watch as a range of emotions dances upon her face—awe, curiosity, trepidation, and joy. I tap her nose lightly and smile at her soothingly as she looks up at me. She smiles back bashfully and quickly turns away from me to continue analyzing her surroundings. Meanwhile, Rachel has her eyes locked straight ahead as she focuses on the paved road, almost as stoic and alert as her mother.

I'm not a world traveler, by any means, but my heart fills with passion and longing when I find myself surrounded by forestry and creeks. A primal urge takes hold of me, almost like this is the environment in which I'm meant to thrive.

I think back to a memory that I have of sliding steadily down a slope in Tennessee in order to reach the bed of a creek. Once there, almost on instinct, I burst into a sprint and ran alongside the creek—dodging fallen limbs, following curves in the creek, and ducking beneath hanging branches. That is one of my most valued memories, and it comes to my mind so frequently as one of the purest feelings of joy that I have ever felt.

I blush. I'm somewhat jealous that many others in the world have scenery like this at every turn. Almost simultaneously, I'm frustrated that they likely take it for granted.

I begin to get nervous as we near the top. From the base of the hill, the road hadn't seemed steep, but as we reach the peak, a gravitational pull begins to engulf me.

Briefly, I feel as if I'm on a roller coaster, especially as Julia takes a sudden sharp left turn off the road and onto the edge of the cliff. She begins to drive off the path and onto the long grass. She continues driving, and I slowly watch the lake creep into view and quickly realize why she detoured from the main road. From this height, I can see the entire campground fanning out around the lake, bustling with activity. She travels a short distance before stopping the golf cart rather forcefully.

"This is amazing," I whisper as I look out over the lake.

Rather than find the words to speak, I study every detail. The grass is lush at the base of the woods, and the roots from the trees wind their way out from the forest and onto what I can only refer to as a gnarled path. Off-road vehicles seem to have created the route ahead of us instead of it being paved like the one we detoured from. Ruts have formed within the grass to give way to a compacted dirt road, one third the size of a vehicle.

Three feet from the path, the lush greenery resumes until it disappears over the cliff's edge. Beyond the cliff I see the lake, sparkling in the light of the setting sun. The lake's surface is sprinkled with boats, and smaller canoes peacefully glide along the edges. Spots for the campers extend in vertical rows away from the shore, some of them with guests arriving and offloading. If I strain my eyes, I can just barely make out children riding bikes on the roads far below.

"Now, you see, this is why we come here." Julia smiles smugly.

"I honestly can't get over the fact this is so close to home and that we didn't have to travel for hours to get here," I respond.

"I guess you don't get out much," she says bluntly.

I raise one eyebrow and look at her with a hint of contempt. I let the remark slide. It isn't the first bold remark she has made toward me, and I know it won't be the last. I would like to blame it on the pregnancy, but she is, and will always be, unapologetically herself.

My mother's words chime in my head yet again, "Kill 'em

with kindness." I shake the grimace off my face quickly and turn to smile at her.

"I'm so happy that you guys wanted to share this with us. This is the absolute best! Is it a good idea for us to drive over all those roots?" I direct my gaze forward and nod in the direction of the roots that sporadically encroach upon the dirt path.

I ask on behalf of the baby in her belly, and she must realize my innuendo because she places her hand on her belly and says, "Yep, the baby will be fine, and the girls will love it!"

"Girls, isn't this *so* cool?" I ask them. Our little ones don't talk much, but I still like to include them. They smile at me and point at the lake.

"Look at all that water down there!" I say with excitement.

They begin to become restless and attempt to start wiggling down and out, so Julia says, "Hold on, girls. Let's get back to it."

Chapter Four

Brooke

Then

We both reposition the kids on the seat between us before we start the golf cart up again. Julia begins to drive us alongside the cliff, surprisingly with more than enough room so that I feel safe rather than in danger of falling.

The golf cart bounces periodically when we hit large roots, and as we drive through the potholes that litter the ground, a bend forms ahead along the path, taking us into the woods and away from the view of the lake.

Julia stomps her foot on the pedal as we come away from the edge of the cliff, and we begin to race through the forest instead. We ride along in silence, slowing intermittently in order to avoid low-hanging branches or overgrown brush that impedes our intended route.

Eventually, we come upon a fork in the path behind the charred remains of a long-extinguished fire. The path on the right leads into more trees, while the one to the left appears to lead us back closer to the edge that overlooks the lake. She slows down and steers the golf cart toward the latter route and comes to a halt shortly afterward. Here, the vibrant green trees appear to form a picture frame in which the lake, once again, is the masterpiece in the center.

"We always take a picture right here when we come," Julia says to me. "We'll wait for Yasmin to get here so we can come back and all take it together."

I nod in understanding.

"Hey, girls, want to explore?" I ask the kids, and they look up at me with expressions of delight.

I look at Julia to confirm that it is okay. She nods, and I step off the golf cart. I lift Erin off the seat first and onto the ground then Rachel right after that. Julia remains seated on the golf cart.

"This is such a neat little place to get away," I say. "Tucked into the woods but still with a great view of the lake."

"Oh, yeah, and the last time we were here, we didn't get to enjoy it for long. When we came for our picture, there was a group of guys sitting around that fire, actually," she says as she points back to the fork in the road. "It wasn't really a big deal, but it looked like a bachelor trip or something, so we took the picture and went on our way."

"I really like this. It's like a scene from a movie or a famous painting," I say as I examine the trees that frame the lake.

"The lake is great, but it's kind of ridiculous because they hardly have any fish in there." She laughs.

"Wait, aren't the guys going fishing tomorrow?" I ask in disbelief, and she laughs at my inquiry.

"They go fishing every time. They wake up early, stay out there for hours, and they literally have never caught a fish," she explains to me. "They don't do it for the purpose of putting food on the table. They use it as the perfect excuse to get outside, away from the women and kids, to all hang out."

I imagine that when she says "they," she is referring to all the people and couples she and Jacob have come here with in the past. That is one thing I have noticed about my neighbors. They don't do anything by themselves. For instance, they'll boil seafood, and they'll invite everyone over. Sometimes, Jacob's mom will even volunteer to keep Rachel, and instead of going out on a date alone, they ask us if we are free. Get a camping site for the weekend somewhere? They try to convince anyone else who has a camper that they should join them. It's a pattern.

"Wow," I say, "they're geniuses. We can't get ahold of them if they're on the boat in the middle of the lake, and we can't be mad if they claim they are trying to catch dinner."

I shake my head at this revelation as I watch the girls pull leaves off the branches in the bushes. I scurry over quickly to make sure there is no poison ivy before quickly realizing that I don't even know what poison ivy looks like. I think it's red, and I don't see any red, so I guess they'll be fine. Just to be safe, I ask Julia.

"Do you see any poison ivy around here?"

"No, I think they try to keep that under control since they know people come through here by foot."

I hope that she is right and not just making an assumption.

Erin digs something out of the dirt, and as I walk over to take it from her, she puts it in her mouth. She does this with almost anything that she finds, which is why I was walking over to try to grab it. As I pull it from her, I'm glad to see it's only an old nickel, but I suddenly become paranoid and quickly realize it could have been a needle or a broken glass bottle. I throw the coin to the side and say, "All right, let's see what this place has to offer."

I carry Erin back to the golf cart and slide her onto the seat, then I walk back to get Rachel, who has wandered even farther away. I walk back to the golf cart, put Rachel next to Erin, and grab the "Oh, shit" handle to hoist myself up. Almost as soon as my butt hits the seat, Julia presses the accelerator, and the golf cart lurches ahead.

We ride for another thirty or so yards at a gradual decline before we reach a gated entry. The gate is open, and a sign nearby reads Primitive Camping.

Julia slows the cart as we enter the gate. As I would imagine, there is no one here. I see no tents, only a building devoted to amenities, like showers and restrooms, in the center of open space.

"Huh, maybe we should have brought the tents. We would have had this whole place to ourselves," Julia says as we drive through. I nod in agreement, recognizing that we both aren't cut out for primitive camping, especially with young children in tow.

"We keep going slowly downhill. I don't know if you noticed," she says to me as I look ahead and see that the farther we go, the closer we get to what seems to be a swampy area.

"The lake cuts through right here," she continues as she points to the stagnant water settling a few yards below the path, "and this is how the people who camp out here get access to the lake."

"This is pretty neat," I say, realizing this is what I saw and speculated about earlier from the base of the hill. "Especially if you put your tent right on the bank," I tell her. No sooner do the words leave my mouth than we catch sight of the tops of a few small modernized white tents down a dip in the land leading to the bank.

She pulls the golf cart into what appears to be a parking spot and exclaims, "Wow, this is so cool! This wasn't here when we came last time."

We all climb out of the golf cart because the only way to reach the tents is to walk down the steep embankment by foot. Julia leads the way, Rachel behind her, and I trail, holding Erin, afraid that she will fall down the steep slope.

"Check this out. It's just the basics! You can rent these for the weekend!" she says excitedly as she points at the informative sign at the entry to the tent.

The tent is the size of a room, with a locked mesh opening so that we can see inside but can't enter. I peer inside, and there is only a bed, a chair, a trash can, and a canister for water. "This is so neat. I wish they had stuff like this when I was younger!" I say as I show Erin the tent.

"I love how it's right on the water too. Although maybe that isn't great since that water is so still. It's probably full of mosquitoes here at night," Julia says as she looks out over the murky and secluded quagmire.

I put Erin down on the ground, and she walks toward the water, near where Rachel is already standing. The water makes me nervous, so I watch them as we talk.

"I'd say we could do this next time, but it would be impossible with kids."

"Who says?" Julia retorts. "They'll be fine. People do it all the time," she reassures me.

"I guess what I'm saying is we can do it, but I don't know if I want to do it." I laugh, embarrassed. "Just the thought of all the bugs, wild animals, water nearby, and the distance it takes to get to the bathroom... not to mention having to be responsible for children. It just doesn't sound appealing to me," I say as I shrug.

"I get that, but we could totally do it."

"Perhaps," I say to appease her.

I pull out my phone, and I take a few pictures of the girls playing along the bank.

"We can just keep riding through and see a few more things before we make our way back," Julia says to me.

She is probably right, since it's almost dark, the remnants of the sun casting a vivid shade of indigo at the base of the falling night sky. We begin to make our way back up the slope and to the golf cart. She leads Rachel back up, and I hitch Erin onto my hip to carry her. As we arrive at the golf cart, I observe an old green Chevy that I am confident wasn't there previously.

"Looks like we wouldn't be the only ones here after all," I say to Julia as we leave the primitive camping ground, exiting out another gate opposite from the way we entered. Through this gate, we find ourselves back on the main road.

"Oh, so this is the same road as earlier. So if we go left, it would take us back?" I ask Julia as she turns down the paved road to the right. She nods and continues driving.

The road has dense forest on either side as we travel farther away. We pass a wide entryway on the right. Through the opening, I see a clearing and a large wooden sign, although I can't quite tell what it says.

"That's the entry to some archery lanes," Julia explains to me, answering for me what's likely displayed on that sign.

As we ride, I take note of small openings into the forest that look like we could traverse in the golf cart if we wanted to. We continue to drive, and I see Erin is becoming drowsy as she fights her heavy eyelids from closing.

Suddenly, my eyes are drawn to a brightly colored sign on the right, with a winding road behind it that leads to an unfamiliar destination.

Camp Sunshine.

"What's that?" I ask inquisitively as I point to the winding road that lies behind the sign.

"Not sure. Probably a summer camp?"

I acknowledge by nodding as a car approaches us from the road beyond the sign.

"That gate is usually locked, so we have never even been down there," she continues.

I give her a look of disappointment as she drives by without stopping or turning down the road to investigate. After it seems like we've traveled past a mile's worth of trees, we come to a large roundabout lined with cabins.

"Oh, this is neat!" I exclaim as it becomes apparent that all the cabins are occupied.

"Oh yeah, people love to rent these out, and it's hard to find a weekend that they have one available," she explains to me as we make our way around the roundabout and start to head back the way we came.

I nudge Erin to keep her from falling asleep, and I whisper into her ear, "Almost back, baby."

I realize as she glances toward me and rubs her eyes that we've begun to turn back at just the right moment. Not only is Erin sleepy, but it seems that darkness has quickly fallen down over the campground like a curtain. Julia turns on the golf cart's headlights as we drive. We fly past the primitive campsites, which means we are now on the portion of the road that I haven't seen yet. More trees line the streets, with entryways where smaller off-road vehicles appear to have traveled.

"We can explore more tomorrow! Every time we come, we find something new around here," Julia says as we reach the crest of the hill and begin our descent toward the lake.

"Does the lake have a name?" I ask.

"Mm-hmm, Lake Pleasant."

We pass the ditch, which I only know is there from the faint trickling sound I hear because the darkness has engulfed everything. Not even the moon provides enough illumination for us to see the road ahead. We pass the boat launch, which has quieted since night fell, and soon find ourselves back at the camper. Another car sits in the grass alongside our vehicles.

"Yay, Yasmin and Bruce finally made it!" Julia shrieks as she swerves the golf cart into the grass, right up to the picnic table set up alongside the camper.

The four of us get out of the golf cart and rush toward the door to welcome the new arrivals.

Chapter Five

Brooke

Now

All I did was scream at first. I try not to do it as much now, but sometimes I can't help it. I don't talk anymore. Something inside stops me. I'm sad. I have so many regrets, and I constantly mourn the life that I thought I had for myself. All that time, wasted. That's what hurts me the most. College—years of learning for nothing. My relationship, my marriage—all the fighting, the resolutions, the great times, and even the worst times... gone. Even now, the years continue to drag on, squandered. So many years have passed. Who knows how many more years are to come, and I can't do anything about it. I can't even try. Too much time has passed, and that metaphorical ship has sailed.

I start to laugh hysterically. It's funny. It has to be because if not, it just hurts.

An image of my daughter appears in my mind. It's hard to remember what she looks like, but the mental image of her is all I have. It is excruciating that the thought of her is the only thing that can calm me and enrage me, simultaneously. Every time that she pops into my mind, I smile and lavish the thought of her briefly before reality rushes forward. When it does, I do anything—and I truly mean anything—to cease the thoughts that follow.

Instead, I count the tiles. I count threads. I tap my fingers. I bang my head against the bed frame, so much so that they've removed it and placed my mattress on the floor. I repeat the alphabet, list all the states in the USA, and when I'm lucky, I lose myself in a book. Another semblance of the life I used to have.

I rarely read because it reminds me of the life that I lost, the kind of life I will never again grasp. My thoughts, they appear lucid, and they are a constant reminder that I can no longer have my daughter. They rage through my head just as quickly as her image does. It hurts, this unending torture.

I can no longer treat patients. I will never again walk along the beach with my husband. Never will I see the aurora borealis.

I scream now, as loud and as long as my voice allows it. Another reason I don't say much—I don't have the voice after years of abusing it.

I rarely talk. Instead, I listen. Listen to all the gossip. The accusations. The truths. The lies. I perceive everything, even though I never respond or acknowledge. I am numb, or at least I try to be. The medication dulls me, and even still I numb myself further from emotions, from feelings. It's how I cope.

But it can't stop the truth, can't erase the past, or numb me completely. So all I do is continue to listen, and I hear them all talk, and I mean I hear everything. Like how the janitor provides contraband for a monetary fee, the guard touches himself while in the blind spots of the security cameras, and they say that the woman across the hall killed her baby. What do they say about me? Oh, I hear that too.

"Beware of that one. She bites."

"She always has that look in her eye."

"She murdered her friend."

"She's the one that screams every night."

"She has no remorse. She feels nothing, not even regret."

I still don't understand, after all this time. I would never hurt anyone. It's not in my character, not in my nature, to cause harm. They never believed me, and I've been so out of my mind that I can't even try to convince them.

Facts are facts. Despite my drenched appearance, I was still covered in blood and dirt when I showed up. I was the last one seen with her. No other suspects, and there was no evidence otherwise to prove that it was anyone but me.

I tried to tell them that we weren't alone, but they say there's no proof anyone else was there. I know the rain made sure of that. The facts also indicate that no one was staying there that night, not from what they can tell anyway. Even now I'm convinced, after all this time, it must have been me. I did it.

Sometimes I rationalize—maybe it wasn't me?

That thought always ends the same. With me slumping my shoulders in defeat as I realize that I can't do anything from a cell. So I sit and I languish instead, alone in my brightly lit cell, square tiles above and below and plain beige walls lined with barred windows and the damage I've inflicted during my imprisonment. The light that shines through the steel bars is a punishment in itself, a constant reminder of the sunshine and the rain. I'll never again indulge in the heat radiating through my skin or the raindrops exploding as they bombard my skin. All my experiences, forever tainted by my actions. No, my inaction.

Although for my relatively good behavior as of late, I'm told I may be eligible for a reward of sorts. Some of the patients here attend a day program. They say that they do crafts, sing songs, attend group seminars and even individual ones. I know that I deserve it, just as much as I know that I don't. I've just about given up, and after all these years, I am on the cusp of acceptance. This is the life I have now. Remembering, denying, redirecting, screaming, crying, and hopefully soon... accepting.

Chapter Six

Brooke

Then

"Hey!" Bruce shouts as we enter through the camper's door. Yasmin approaches us quickly, scooping up Rachel in her arms, and proceeds to squeeze her and spin her around in circles. Rachel giggles, and Yasmin hands her to Bruce, saying, "Our little RayRay is here!" referring to Rachel's nickname. Yasmin then picks up Erin and plants a kiss on her cheek. Julia and I bypass the introductory hugs and sit at the table. Yasmin and Bruce sit on the couch with the kids, and Kent and Jacob get up from the table and go stand near the door.

"Well, I'm out. Too many people here," Jacob jokes.

Bruce gets up and walks over to the guys, and they all start talking about a viral video about a boat or something. I watch the kids play with Yasmin, and I'm so thankful that she loves them like they are her own.

Yasmin and Bruce not only don't have any kids, but they also have no relation to us or our neighbors. Jacob and Bruce have been friends for years, so of course, as a result, Julia and Yasmin became close friends as well. The men were even roommates at one time.

I've only known Yasmin for a short while, but she and Julia get along like sisters. Not in the sense that they look alike, though, as Yasmin has long dark wavy hair and high cheekbones that elevate her features. I mean in the way that they fight like sisters—nothing physical, just catty and judgmental of one another. They even get jealous of things the other has and have full-blown arguments. Which, personally, I don't understand. I'm not that type of person, I guess, as I avoid confrontation at all costs.

Just this last weekend, for example, we were at Julia's house next door and Jacob complimented me for working out. Julia had skipped that day, as she was experiencing a serious bout of morning sickness. I shrank into a corner as Julia started to get upset, and I let her focus all of her anger on her husband.

If he had complimented Yasmin instead of me, she wouldn't have been able to hide from Julia's rage. Julia would have fussed at them both. She and Julia have a deeper relationship because of the years they've spent together, so their altercations are taken more seriously. Just like sisters, they make up eventually, and everything goes back to normal.

Unlike Julia and Jacob, I haven't known Yasmin and Bruce for nearly as long, so I'm not as close to them. I really enjoy their company, especially Yasmin. I feel like she and I have a lot in common. We are both in healthcare, we both love to read, and she has a placid demeanor, much like the one I try to exemplify.

Bruce seems pretty intelligent, and it's not just because he wears glasses. He often provokes thoughtful conversations, which is something I can appreciate these days because I often feel individuals lack not only knowledge but analytical thinking.

I may forget food in the oven on occasion, but I also like to have meaningful discussions, which I'm sometimes able to have with Bruce.

I smile at Yasmin's interaction with the girls, but I'm also smiling at myself in general. These people are a group of friends that I didn't know I needed. I have friends—best friends—but they have lives to live and things that get in the way. It's different with neighbors, as they don't have an excuse to blow you off. So we end up spending time with them and their friends, and I wouldn't want it any other way. It wasn't always this easy to accept, especially when I'd rather sit at home in the shadows and play on my phone. Realistically, these are the moments I'll cherish, and it's better for me to be present in them rather than distracted. Seriously, I'm not going to think back and remember the times I sat on the couch and watched videos and mindlessly scrolled social media posts.

"What are we doing inside?" asks Julia before continuing without a response. "We're camping! Let's go light a fire!"

I stand up and follow everyone outside, waiting at the foot of the stairs to help the girls climb down. I take a seat on one of the chairs placed around the fire pit and think about how I could enjoy myself a lot more inside the camper. At least inside I didn't have to keep a vigilant eye on the children, but now I will because of the fire, moving vehicles, and bugs. The men get to work starting the fire, and my husband brings me a drink. I thank him with a peck on the cheek, and I realize at this moment that I've never seen Jacob and Julia kiss.

I make a funny face and begin to search my memories because surely I'm mistaken? They must have, since they have one child and another on the way, but generally they aren't very affectionate toward one another. I chastise myself internally

There is no need for me to judge and compare relationships, yet I find myself beginning to do so. Yes, my husband may kiss me, but I'm sure Julia and Yasmin's husbands do things for them that mine doesn't do for me. Kent is not perfect, as we fight and nag on occasion. No one has the perfect relationship. We have come a long way, though, and for that I am grateful.

I push comparisons out of my head and instead start to listen to Julia and Yasmin's conversation.

"We can go for a ride tomorrow. Take our annual picture. Maybe bring the girls to the playground," Julia says.

"Playground? I didn't see a park. Here?" I ask, confused.

"Oh, it's here. Somewhere hidden behind all these trees." Yasmin says with a laugh.

"Well, that's neat. I never even saw it," I say and shrug.

Yasmin smiles and says, "Don't get your hopes up because it isn't much. It's an older one, too, so if you go at the wrong time of the day, like when the sun is out, the plastic will literally burn your skin."

I grimace at her statement.

"We could go early, except I like to sleep in. But technically, I have to get up whenever my alarm goes off," I say as I point to Erin, and they laugh.

The fire is ablaze, flames dancing on the wind as we help the kids make s'mores. I eat two of the delectable treats myself. We all sit around the fire, laughing and talking. From the corner of my eye, I see Rachel grab Erin's hair and pull. I let Julia scold her, as it is her child, after all.

"Have you been feeling the baby kick?" asks Yasmin as she leans in to touch Julia's belly.

"A little, especially when I eat chocolate." She laughs as she takes a bite of her third s'more.

I joyfully recall those moments from my own pregnancy—very little morning sickness, a wonderfully easy pregnancy, and pure excitement and awe whenever I felt my baby move in my belly.

I cast my eyes down at my watch to check the time, and I realize that I usually have Erin in bed by now. I'm surprised she hasn't fallen asleep yet, especially after our golf cart adventure earlier.

"I know Rachel is a night owl, but it's about time for me to put Erin down," I say as I get up from my chair. I pick up Erin from the ground, and I walk her around to everyone to deliver good night kisses.

Once I've given her a bird bath and I have her in her pajamas, we lie down on the bottom bunk in our room. It's still too early for me to settle down, so I'll probably go back outside once I get Erin to fall asleep.

Although the lights are off, I can see her clearly, and I stare mesmerized as her eyelids begin to fall. My baby, my sweet girl, my world. I admire her button nose, her flushed cheeks, her unruly blond hair, and her pursed lips. I love everything about her, often thinking to myself how lucky I am. Her father and I were together for ten years before we tried to have a baby. It's a miracle that, of all the babies that our DNA could have combined to create, we wound up with the best one.

I gently remove my arm from behind her neck and lower her onto the bed. I softly kiss her forehead and stand back to ensure that I didn't wake her. Exiting the room, I head outside the camper into what is sure to be a playful evening with friends.

Chapter Seven

Brooke

Then

I hear noises outside our room, and I am reluctant to open my eyes and start the day. I immediately think about Erin and turn my head to the side to make sure she is there. She is, but I don't breathe a sigh of relief until I see her chest rise and fall. There it is. Good, she is alive.

I close my eyes again and think about the restless night that I had. My husband's snoring, paired with the camper shaking, had my nerves on edge. Unusual for me because I usually sleep hard and undisturbed.

Last night, when it was finally time for bed and I attempted to get settled in our room, all I could pay attention to was how much the camper seemed to shake when anyone moved a muscle. Lying in bed, looking up at the ceiling, I remembered that they propped that boulder up to stabilize the camper. Immediately, my anxiety took hold, and my thoughts began to frenzy.

What if the boulder loosened with all the shaking, and the

camper fell down the small hill it sits on and into the lake below?

Of course, when I finally fell asleep, I was awakened by Kent getting into bed beside me. The guys decided last minute, right before bedtime, to embark on a nighttime boat ride. I don't even know what time they got back.

It's not out of the ordinary for them to do that. Such is the life of a good ol' boy from southern Louisiana. Why stay home when there are numerous waterways to explore, muddy lily pads to drive through, and countless bullfrogs to catch and eat?

The rest of the night wasn't any better. I was awoken intermittently by Kent's snoring, which caused me to reposition myself, making the camper shake, again igniting my anxiety.

As I stare at the bunk bed above us, I say a prayer of thanks that we didn't slide down the hill and meet our demise overnight. I take a deep breath in and pull myself out of bed as Erin begins to stir. Kent is already gone from the bed, which is not unusual as he's always been an early riser. I scoop Erin up into my arms, and I open the door to see that everyone is already awake. Guess all the noise was to ensure that we, too, would soon wake up to start the day.

I walk into a chorus of good mornings, and Julia directs me to fix my coffee as we wait for Bruce to finish cooking breakfast. I place Erin down, and as I make my coffee, I think back to last night and how much fun we had before I tried to go to sleep. As I stand, waiting for my coffee to finish brewing, I inhale the bitter smell and allow it to sharpen my senses as I think back to last night.

It was so refreshing to drink and gossip with friends while Erin and Rachel slept peacefully inside, unable to interrupt. It was one of those nights one has with friends, the kind where everyone talks about anything and everything. The most random things allowed to be said, knowing no judgment will be passed.

At one point Julia brought up how she once thought about bringing her dog to eat a hibachi dinner, which made us all burst into laughter, thinking of a large yellow Labrador patiently sitting at a hibachi table.

It was a nice night until Jacob responded, which he claimed was in jest, to Yasmin's statement about how she almost couldn't find someone to watch her cat. He laughed and told Yasmin that he would take care of her cat any time, and that was when Julia flew off the handle. The lively conversation ended shortly after that, with all the ambiance extinguished. Jacob and Julia ventured inside to argue briefly before he stormed out and convinced the guys to leave for a ride in the boat.

I glance toward Julia as I sit next to her on the sofa. I look at her, hoping to gain insight on whether their disagreement was resolved last night, but her sour look suggests that they may still be upset with one another. She doesn't acknowledge my glance, and her shoulders are stiff, making her appear aloof as she stares down at the kids playing with toys on the floor. I mean, look at how sweet their play is. How is she not smiling? Actually, she seems rather distracted, almost as if she is looking through them and not at them.

"So, what is the plan for the day?" I ask the group.

Kent shrugs, but Julia perks up then and says, "I think we girls are going to go off and explore after breakfast."

Jacob looks at her briefly but says nothing. It's like he's watching her with disdain. Well, that is, before he clears his grimace, quickly replacing it with a smirk. I avert my eyes. Typically, they get over things rather fast and don't hold grudges toward one another. I really hope all this doesn't last and that we can avoid an awkward weekend.

Chapter Eight

Brooke

Now

I pry my eyes open. I'm always scared here, and the fog is constantly lingering at the edge of all my thoughts. Occasionally, it breaks, and I can process my thoughts and distract myself. A vast majority of the time, though, the overwhelming shroud is here to stay. I often find myself on autopilot, coasting through the motions. Existing, and nothing more. I do what they tell me to do. I choke down the medicines they make me take. It's easier that way. I find solace in the dullness brought to my senses. Why do I even bother opening my eyes? I shut them again.

The one emotion that is constant, the one I am desperate to weaken, is regret. Regret that we went out that night. Regret for what I did. Regret for what I didn't do. Regret that I couldn't keep my shit together long enough to save myself and my future. Regret that I don't try harder to free myself. Regret for all of it.

Every day here is the same, or at least it always seems that way.

Nothing ever changes. Even the staff is always the same—no fresh faces. The food is always the same, both in taste and appearance. The medicine—always the same pills. The regret that will never dissipate. Wash. Rinse. Repeat. I deserve this, though, don't I?

This morning, like every morning, I lie in bed, fighting a war against my thoughts.

I hate that I feel this way. I never was this type of person, or at least I didn't think that I was. I used to be so optimistic. So happy and so lively. I'm a husk of the woman that I used to be.

I'd rather be dead and buried than live through another dull, repetitious day. Instead of being buried in dirt, I'm stuck here, buried in sins.

Buried in guilt.

Buried by action.

Buried by inaction.

"Brooke, let's get you ready early. You've got to catch the bus with the others," someone says suddenly from the mist.

My eyes burst wide open as I track the voice to my doorway. This is new. This is not a part of the hell I've come to know. I sit up quickly, or as quickly as my dulled senses allow me to move.

I stare at her questioningly, my forehead raised and my eyebrows scrunched. Surely she doesn't mean me. I'm afraid that she's in the wrong room. As I rarely speak, I forgo words and instead continue to deliver my stare, hoping it conveys my question adequately enough.

"Yes, dear. You," she says with a smile. "If you're feeling up to it, we can get you ready early. That will give you time for a quick breakfast before we go."

I freeze. I don't deserve this. Maybe I do. Maybe it's a trap, and that's something that my past actions merit. Maybe this outing will be even worse than the hell I've been entombed in.

I've never spoken to anyone about the day program and what it entails, but I have heard things. I imagine that's where they plan to take me. I've heard more positives than negatives, though. I have to give it a chance. Since I do everything else they make me do, I might as well go along with this charade as well.

In response, I don't smile. I don't move. Instead, I look at the orderly with a blank stare, once again arguing internally with myself. I shake my head and ease myself from the bed. The orderly takes my movement from the bed as my silent agreement, which I suppose it is.

Let's see what this is all about.

Chapter Nine

CJ

Then

I'm not sure why Dad decided to spring this father-son trip on me all of a sudden. It's not like I'm a fishing enthusiast. I can hardly rig up my own line, and waiting for the fish to bite the hook is beyond boring. Alas, here we are. Sitting in a small boat on a huge lake, with tall trees everywhere. Well, we are technically in a large lake but tucked away in a small pocket of stagnant water. The breeze doesn't seem to penetrate the trees here, and sweat beads on my forehead, causing me to wipe it away in order to keep it from getting into my eyes. This is not how I expected to spend my weekend since this isn't something we usually do. Especially randomly, with no pretense, no warning.

Man, this was so random. I got home from my friend's house earlier today, and Dad already had my bags packed. Even weirder, my mom was there.

They're divorced and haven't lived together in years. I looked at her questioningly before he told me to give her a kiss and get in the truck. He didn't seem too excited about it, though. Pretty sure she's making him spend time with me. She's hoping some quality time will fix my attitude. Her words, not mine.

Guess that would explain Dad's behavior. This probably wasn't even his idea.

I see my cork bob, and I start to reel in my catch. As the cork gets closer to the boat, I peer through the murky green water, but I don't see anything on the hook. My bait remains intact too. I pull it all the way out of the water to determine that I have caught a big ol' serving of nothing. I cast again, aiming for the same spot, hoping to catch the same fish this time around.

"That was probably just grass on the line," my dad mumbles without looking at me.

I roll my eyes. He has no faith in me. For someone who tends to put so much faith in everyone else, it's almost like he has nothing left for me. I feel like that's why I'm here. This is a sorry attempt at bonding. Well, I've got news for him. It's too late. Good thing I'll be eighteen soon enough. Just ten more agonizing months, and I'll be an official adult and out of the house and on my own. No looking back for me. I don't mesh with my parents. We are so different, and I can't stand living under either of their roofs.

Dad spends all day helping others, but he can't tell that I need help. What kind of bullshit is that? How can he rescue others and leave me behind without any consideration?

Mom is no better. She cares more about her hobbies and interests than she does mine—or about me in general.

I mean, like, I know they love me. Or that they love that sweet kid I used to be. But they've got to realize I'm going to be my own person one day. Instead, they fight me on every decision that I make. All we do is argue because they're never happy with anything I do.

Just a little while longer. Then I'm free to make all my own decisions, and there's nothing they can do to stop me.

Money? Not a problem. That's what credit cards are for, right?

House? I've got older friends with their own places who'll let me crash there.

College? Nah, not for me. I can get a job without it. I'm sure there's something out there that I can do. At this point, anything will be better than the life I have now.

Man, maybe Dad was right, and I just caught grass earlier. Still no bite.

It's possible that this fishing thing is good. It's so quiet out here, and I can start to plan for my future. Plan my great escape. I honestly don't even think they'll chase after me. I think they'll let me walk out that door, shaking their heads, claiming that they tried their best but that it wasn't enough. That hurts, though. I'm their only child. Can they really be so callous as to let me walk out of their lives? Shit, they don't try now, so why would they try when I go to leave?

It's always "You could do better," "Use your damn head," "One day you'll appreciate everything we've done for you," and "You're so useless sometimes."

But it's never "You're so good at guitar," or "Thanks for cleaning your bathroom," or "We can't wait to see the things you'll accomplish."

I see other kids with their parents. They've got totally different relationships. Their parents seem kind, caring, and compassionate. Meanwhile, it's like my parents want to return me because I wasn't what they ordered. Sometimes, I give them the benefit of the doubt and think that maybe all kids feel like this at some point. But then the harsh words come slamming back and I know it's just me, alone in this world.

I bet they even blame me for their divorce, and that's why they're so hateful. Although I'm sure Mom's constant nagging and Dad's affair didn't help their marriage. I'll show them. They think I'm that bad? Oh man, just wait. I'm getting more and more upset the longer I sit here.

The next ten months are going to be torture for them. Like some next-level, maniacal shit. I'll do whatever I want, when I want.

Punish me? I don't care. I won't listen.

Toothbrushes? In the toilet.

Late for work? Flat tire, courtesy of yours truly.

After my farewell tour, I'll be gone. Leaving them wishing they had treated me better and also relieved to have me gone. Good. Maybe they won't chase after me, and they'll leave me be. Yep, that's the plan.

I'm just starting to really work myself up when I hear the sound of gravel scattering below tires on the bank of this stupid pond we're floating in.

It's so sudden that I turn my head automatically to see where it came from. I see a golf cart entering the campground area where we'll sleep tonight, the one that surrounds the pond we're in. Seems like it's a few women and their kids on a joyride. Huh. I was happy to discover that we were the only ones that seemed to be staying in this part of the campground when we pulled up. It's bad enough that I'll basically have to be sleeping outside with my dad. I don't want to have to add socializing with strangers to this horrible trip.

Just as quickly as I turned my head to see them, I turn it back to look at my cork resting atop the motionless water. I keep my eye on them through my peripheral, though. They've stopped moving and appear to be talking and looking at those fancy tents that are scattered along the bank. It's actually so quiet that I can hear bits of their conversation.

"Yeah, this is neat!" one girl says.

One of the women is following the kids around, keeping them away from the edge of the water, mumbling to them, but I can't hear what she's saying. The last of the three women appears to be looking in our direction. That's when I notice they all start talking together in hushed voices. I wonder if they're talking about us.

I don't have to wonder long, though, because that last one with her hair up in a clip says, "They'll never catch anything in that dingy water. They're wasting their time."

Well, screw you too. Who does she think she is? I move slightly to turn and say something to them, but my dad's foot bumps into mine, and he gives me a look. A look that says "not worth the bullshit" as he tilts his head.

Okay, yeah, I can get behind that. Not worth my effort. Plus, they have kids, and I'd hate to make a scene in front of them. Even though their moms seem like total bitches. Luckily for me, they don't stay long. They take off in the golf cart shortly afterward, and we are left alone once again. I glance at my dad. He's focused on the end of his fishing line and appears to be lost in his thoughts. Now that I think about it, I don't think I've seen him reel in his line at all.

I hope that bitch wasn't right because I'd love nothing more than to catch a fish and know she was wrong.

As if he can hear my thoughts, Dad starts to reel in his line. Either he caught something, or he's ready to give up on catching a fish today. I'm slightly relieved, hoping it's the latter, as my body odor worsens with each minute we remain in the heat. When we're done, maybe I can find a patch of water that isn't filthy and rinse off all the sweat that's accumulated on my skin. While he's reeling in his line, his phone vibrates with a text, and I look down in time to see that it's from Mom.

We both put our phones on top of the tackle box when we began fishing because Dad told me we should focus on the fish for the weekend. He actually sounded a little sincere when he told me earlier, "No distractions. That way, we can spend some quality time together."

I scoff, now thinking about it. If that's the case, then why is Mom texting him? Not to mention, they're divorced, and as far as I'm concerned, they shouldn't be talking at all.

The text preview is still showing on the screen, and I look at Dad to make sure he isn't paying attention before I try to read the text from Mom.

But I'm too late. The screen's black again when I look back. What the hell was that about? Maybe this weekend will be interesting after all.

Chapter Ten

Brooke

Then

This morning, after we finished breakfast, Julia, Yasmin, and I decided to ride up the hill with the kids on the golf cart to see everything in the early-morning sun. Julia was excited to show Yasmin the primitive tents that were now available for rent. They both talked in jest about how fun it would be to come back when it was cooler, likely later this year. I smiled along in agreement as they made plans, still unsure if I'd accompany them.

We saw a couple of men fishing from a johnboat in the small grotto as we were leaving. Julia watched them with scrutiny and said, "They'll never catch anything in that dingy water. They're wasting their time."

Much to our dismay, her words appeared to echo atop the water. I grimaced and looked away, hoping that the men in the small boat didn't hear what she said.

The beautiful spot where our friends always take their annual picture was pretty close to the back entrance for the primitive camping area, so we ducked off to take their picture shortly after that. I felt honored when they asked me and Erin to jump in instead of keeping me behind the camera. We set the phone up on an automatic timer, and we took the sweetest picture in front of that beautiful view.

After that, we left the primitive campgrounds and brought the girls to the empty playground. It was early enough in the day that the plastic wasn't scalding and had not yet been scorched by the sun. We stayed until a small drizzle found its way above us. It wasn't an outright downpour, but we used it as an excuse to get the girls to want to leave.

Now, back at the campsite, we're letting the girls nap while we snack on cookies outside the camper. Julia and I are playing on our phones. I'm still limited to what I can do, though, as I hardly have any service and my social media pages won't refresh with new posts.

"Dang, phone. I swear, every time I leave Louisiana, my cell phone service disappears," I say aloud to no one in particular.

"Mine works fine," Julia says without looking up from her phone.

So much for our device-free weekend. I turn mine off and look up since I have nothing better to do, and instead I relish the fact that we can see the lake down the hill.

The camping spots here are separated generously from one another, which is nice because I find it's easy to feel crowded when one goes camping. We must have really quiet neighbors because I haven't heard or seen them since we arrived.

I turn my head away from the lake and toward the road to see a man walking by in pants and a hoodie. I watch him inquisitively. It's rather hot outside to go for a walk in an outfit like that. I mean, everyone is allowed to make their own choices, but it's not the ideal outfit for this sweltering heat. When I was younge like he appears to be, I used to dress like that, too, so I can't b too judgmental. Nevertheless, he continues on, not sparing m a glance.

I hear muffled laughter and look up as the golf cart emerge into view. Our husbands pull up quickly, and as Kent is gettin out, he asks me, "Where's Erin?"

"Yasmin is inside with the girls, putting them down for nap," I say sweetly.

Suddenly, Julia sets her phone down and stares intensely a Jacob before she begins to raise her voice venomously.

"So, even when we're camping and we're supposed to b having family time, you still can't stay here with me and you child?" she demands.

My eyes widen in shock, as she appeared relatively fine unt this moment.

I quickly glance at Kent, consequentially averting my eye from Julia and Jacob. From the corner of my eye, I see Jaco take a defensive stance, crossing his arms over his raised ches

"Seriously?" he asks assertively before continuing. "Wher did that come from, Julia?"

She bends down and picks up her phone from her chair an says, "That's about right. Never one to admit when you'r wrong."

The door to the camper opens, and Yasmin walks out, un aware of the confrontational conversation that just transpire She takes a seat on the now-empty golf cart.

I notice a scuffle on the gravel near the road and divert m attention in time to observe the same hooded figure, no scurrying away, presumably back the way he came.

Yikes, he must have gotten a front-row seat to the derange

scene that just unfolded. No wonder he is fleeing. I would, too, if I could. I look down at my shorts and tank top, once again, pondering why he chose to wear that particular outfit with all this heat and humidity.

Julia's scoff catches my attention as she walks into the camper without saying another word. We all look at one another and shrug.

"Maybe it's the pregnancy hormones?" I suggest.

Jacob laughs at my remark and says, "No, we all know she's always been a bitch."

I am taken aback briefly that he would refer to her like that. Although it isn't the first time I've heard that endearing nickname.

With Julia inside, the five of us continue to converse and discuss the events of the day that we've each had so far.

"It's pretty hot outside," Jacob states about fifteen minutes later.

He then makes eye contact with Yasmin, who is still sitting on the golf cart, and asks her, "Want to go make wind?"

Yasmin seems to consider the offer briefly before nodding in approval, deciding that it would be nice to cool off while cruising around on the golf cart.

"Hey, babe, I'm going ride with Jacob. Be back in a second," Yasmin tells Bruce, blowing him a kiss.

Bruce smiles and continues his conversation with Kent and me as Jacob leaves us to join Yasmin.

I feel a slight disappointment that they didn't invite me, but at the same time, I understand that they probably didn't ask me because they know I'd prefer to be here if Erin wakes up.

Technically, Kent is here and could take care of her, but he doesn't usually because she wakes up so cranky from her naps.

I laugh to myself, doubting that they even thought about all the logistics, especially since Yasmin has no children and Jacob hardly takes care of his own.

The two of them pull out onto the road and drive away.

Chapter Eleven

Brooke

Then

Shortly after they leave, Julia walks out of the camper and sits back in her chair.

"Where did Jacob go?" she asks me, looking confused.

I flinch as I realize that she is not going to like my answer.

"He and Yasmin took the golf cart out to catch the breeze," I say in response to her inquiry.

Julia's face immediately turns red, and her eyes begin to fill with tears.

I clear my throat and say, "I didn't think you would want to go with him since you guys have been arguing all morning."

"I can't believe he didn't even ask me if I wanted to go, especially since Rachel is sleeping and you guys are here to keep an eye on her," she replies. "He legit had the time and the ability to spend time with me, and he didn't even consider it! He chose her!" Julia says, the volume of her voice rising with every word.

She looks at me pleadingly, analyzing my reaction in an

attempt to validate her outburst.

"Really, though," she continues, trying to rationalize her feelings, "yes, we are arguing, but we're arguing because he doesn't spend time with me. So don't you think in order to fix that, he would choose to try to spend time with me?"

I breathe out a sigh of defeat because the fact is that she has a point. It also means that Jacob doesn't have a chance of redeeming himself. There isn't anything else that any one of us could say to aid in Jacob's defense.

Now, I could point out that when I'm upset with someone, the last thing I would want to do is spend time alone with them, but instead, I try to look at the situation from her perspective. The perspective of a neglected wife.

"Hmm. Yes, you're kind of right. You guys never get alone time together, and he just left," I tell her, stoking the fires of her anger.

"That's what I'm saying! I'm his wife, and I'm not even the first thing that he thinks of. He doesn't think about Rachel either. He assumes I'm going to stay here and watch his child. Ahh, the luxury," she says with frustration.

I grit my teeth because there is an element of truth to what she is saying, but I know that if I continue to agree that I'll only make the situation worse. Jacob will be in even deeper trouble when he gets back if I encourage her.

"Well, technically, Yasmin was already sitting on the golf cart. He said he was hot and probably didn't want to be rude and tell her to get off. He wanted to get some cool air." I pause to take a breath and observe her reaction before I continue. "He probably won't be gone long."

Some of the tension falls from Julia's shoulders, and I can see that she wants to accept my response as the most probable explanation. Alas, all she does is purse her lips in thought.

We all continue to sit outside, and time seems to go by slowly. Although I think I was initially able to convince her to go easy on Jacob, I think that the longer he and Yasmin take to come back, the more my efforts will have been in vain.

I can see now by the look on Julia's face that any chance of forgiving Jacob is dissipating with every minute that passes. It's about forty-five minutes later when Julia speaks again to say, "Where the fuck are they?"

My eyes widen, and I look at Kent to gain insight into how to proceed. He and Bruce are immersed in conversation, oblivious to Julia's remark, but their ignorance is short-lived as Julia begins to raise her voice again.

"Is it not super sketchy that they just went off together, have been gone for almost an hour, and no one has heard from them?" she continues on, looking at the guys, seeking confirmation.

She doesn't get it, as they look at her and shrug. Yasmin is Bruce's wife, but he doesn't seem too concerned about the whole thing.

"I drive around this campground all the time, and I can't see them going anywhere that would take this long," she says.

Personally, I've never been here, so I only assumed that they were sightseeing. Even from what I've seen, I could totally understand them being gone for a while. There are so many hidden paths and roads that I haven't traversed yet. I'm not going to argue with her, though. She'll only refocus her anger and attack me instead if I do.

Say she is right, and there are only so many places they could go. What would that mean? Images of Yasmin and Jacob hiding in the woods and making out in the golf cart enter my mind. I don't say anything out loud, though, because I know that would only increase Julia's anger.

I soon realize that I don't have to speak up because I see on her face that she is thinking the same thing. She looks directly at Bruce.

"So you just trust her to go off with another man for an hour," she snarls audaciously before continuing. "That's normal for you guys?"

Bruce shrugs and says, "I'm sure that they got stuck doing something, or they're talking to someone, and it's taking them a little longer to head back."

Bruce must be familiar with this kind of confrontation with Julia because her snide remark doesn't seem to have an impact on him, as he provided a rational excuse quickly in an attempt to appease her. Julia grabs her phone aggressively off the picnic table and calls Jacob.

I only know that she is calling him because shortly after she begins her call, a quacking-duck ringtone interrupts the music playing over the radio. That's when Julia and I both realize that he doesn't have his phone with him and we are listening to his playlist.

The hiccup in her plan doesn't make her falter. She then begins to make another call, presumably to Yasmin. Her phone volume is loud enough for me to hear an endless ringing, but Yasmin doesn't answer. When she glances at me, I shrug.

There is no talking to Julia right now, not with rage and malevolence radiating from her. Nothing that I say can help the situation, especially since I empathize with her. If my husband had free time, I would expect and hope that he would dedicate that time toward me, his wife, and not blatantly choose to spend it with another woman.

I pretend to play on my phone despite not having a strong

enough signal to do anything on it. Since our "device detox" seems to be out the window, I may as well. I'm not bringing up that tidbit right now, though, as I don't want to end up on the wrong side of a debate with Julia.

When I notice a pause in Bruce and Kent's conversation, I join them, attempting to distance myself from the chaos by feigning interest in their discussion about duck hunting.

Time continues to pass, and Julia just sits in her chair, seething. She continuously looks up from her phone and out toward the road. Eventually, we hear the sound of tires on gravel and look up to see Jacob and Yasmin appear in the distance.

I glance at my watch to see that it has been a little over an hour since they left. As the golf cart turns down our road, I mentally prepare for the awkward conversation that is about to transpire.

As soon as Jacob turns off the key to the ignition, Julia asks him, "Where did you go?"

Jacob doesn't yet realize the trouble he is in as he casually responds, "The usual. Just around. Nowhere specific."

"So you're telling me that you just rode around for an hour and didn't stop or do anything purposeful with your time?" she retorts.

"Julia, it was hot. I wanted to make wind," he says defensively.

Although Julia was surprisingly calm until this moment, she unloads on Jacob as he and Yasmin exit the golf cart.

"So you wanted to make wind, and you took Yasmin instead of me... the mother of your child? We literally have the perfect opportunity because said child is sleeping and we have people here to watch her. It blows my mind that you didn't even think to ask me if I wanted to go! Altogether, you vanish, don't invite me, *and* don't tell me before you go and disappear forever!" she yells at Jacob. She pauses briefly to catch her breath before proceeding.

"I don't know why I'm even surprised," she snaps. "Of course you choose to spend time with anyone but me, and to add insult, you chose her."

Yasmin holds her hands up in a defensive motion and says, "Julia, we didn't mean to offend you."

"Yeah, seriously, why are you even acting like this? Everything you're saying makes you sound crazy," Jacob tells Julia.

Julia's eyes ignite with fire at his remark.

"You want to see crazy? You know what? Get back in the golf cart! You're going to show me the exact fucking route that you took, the one that lasted a whole hour!"

Julia proceeds to get into the golf cart, and even though she doesn't ask me to, I barely squeak out in a whisper, "I'll listen for Rachel."

I'm relieved that the two of them will take this confrontation somewhere else and alleviate the tension that's been brewing here since Julia noticed Jacob and Yasmin were gone.

Chapter Twelve

Brooke

Now

As soon as we arrive at the day program, they quickly herd us inside, which I imagine is because of the rain falling down outside in thick sheets. I recognize some others among us, with a few unfamiliar faces mixed in as well. One girl, who I'm pretty sure is named Susan, approaches me.

"Hey, my name's Grace. What's yours?" she asks as she waves a hand.

Oh, I guess I'm mistaken.

I don't respond to her question because I never do. I try to avoid talking, for the most part, because what's the point? So instead, in an attempt to dispel her, I avert my eyes. She continues speaking to me anyway.

"I'll be your tour guide today," she says in an awful accent, which I think is supposed to sound British.

"You don't talk too much, but that's okay because I talk enough for the both of us," she says as she motions for me to follow her down the hall. I follow her, her straight onyx hair bouncing from side to side as she moves forward.

"First, we start with a really easy craft activity since they don't trust us with scissors. Next, we do a group therapy session, where each of us can talk all about our shit, which may I add, I cannot wait to hear what you have to say," she says as she smirks at me over her shoulder. "After that, we take a lunch break before diving into a book reading with a heaping dose of kumbaya."

Grace is talking so fast that she barely takes in a breath before she continues, "Lastly, we each meet separately with the head dog. I say that because they are in charge and they love to get into our heads. So before you go see your dog, or whenever you are done, you just have to chill out and watch TV here in the lobby," she says, looking exhausted from spitting all that out.

"Oh, I almost forgot! Don't try to make a run for it, or they'll shoot you," she says before pausing to stare deeply into my eyes, her eyebrows raised and eyes wide—blank, even.

"Just kidding," she says as she smiles. "Or am I?"

She then walks away, only looking over her shoulder once to ensure that I'm following.

I stand there, though, taking it all in. Grace strikes me as very overstimulating, and I need a second to pull myself back together. I take a deep inhale and begin to follow the others as they shuffle through the dimly lit gray hallway before funneling into a door on the right side.

I find myself in a large room with tables, no chairs, and numerous craft materials located in the center of the room. An almost-sterilized smell permeates the air, and the room appears spotless overall except for the craft supplies at the center. Atop the tables, I see pre-cut shapes, and I wince as I realize Grace wasn't lying about the scissors thing. A rather large lady, with short poofy dark hair and glasses, stands at the center of the room next to the craft table. She begins to explain the activity as she hands out additional materials.

I begin to lose myself in the activity and get to work coloring and composing. When I finish, I admire the wind chime that I've created with a sense of pride, or at least, that's what it feels like. I haven't felt pride in a long time. I then look at the time that is portrayed on the clock in the room. I almost can't believe how much time has passed, and on top of that, I also can't believe that my mind managed to stay focused without wandering.

The lady at the front of the room snaps her fingers and says, "Okay, gang, grab a chair from along the wall and form a circle around me."

I do as she says. Grace places her chair next to mine, but she faces it away from the center of the circle. Grace slumps down in the chair, her back to the center, and she appears agitated with having to be here.

"Susan, you know what I meant. Facing me, please," the woman says, her eyes lingering on Grace's back. Grace turns her chair around begrudgingly. I whip my head to the side and stare at Grace/Susan, expecting her to explain herself, but instead she turns to me and says, "What are you staring at, weirdo?"

I turn my head back toward the center and see that the poofy-haired lady has taken a seat at the apex of the circle and is ready to begin. The woman directs her hand toward Grace/Susan and says, "Maybe you'd like to start, Susan?"

Grace/Susan rolls her eyes.

"I literally do not understand why I am even here. I don't have anything to say, as I don't belong here among the crazies," she retorts as she slouches even deeper into her chair.

The poofy-haired woman averts her eyes from her and instead refocuses them on me and asks, "Brooke?"

I stare at her. I don't want to speak in front of these people. Shit, I don't want to speak to anyone. I have a feeling she will continue to press me if I remain silent, so instead, I begin to scream.

"Whoa, calm down. You don't have to participate yet. I understand this is a big change. We'll move on," she says as she turns in her chair to target another face in the crowd.

I take a deep breath and settle myself. I spend the remainder of the group session listening to the others speak. When we finish, the lady waves at a camera in the corner of the room, and the doors open. A few men come in, and we are asked to stand and line up against the wall.

They begin to rearrange the tables, placing our chairs around them, and then they leave to fetch our lunch trays, I presume. That is, if whatever Grace/Susan told me is to be believed. I move to sit next to her, not to speak to her but to analyze her further. As soon as I sit, she turns toward me and extends her hand.

She offers me a rather bashful glance and says, "Hi, I'm Rebeca. Pleasure to make your acquaintance."

Chapter Thirteen

Brooke

Then

As Julia and Jacob drive off down the road, we all look at each other and shrug. I roll my eyes before I say, "I cannot believe that just happened."

Bruce responds by saying, "Well, honestly, I'm not surprised. This practically always happens. Different scenarios. Same bullshit from Julia."

Yasmin looks confused and asks her husband, "Umm, what did I miss?"

We begin to fill her in about how Julia reacted once she realized Yasmin had left with Jacob. Yasmin doesn't appear surprised or insulted. Her face remains calm as she listens to us all explain the chain of events that followed her departure.

"Has she acted like this toward you before?" I ask Yasmin.

"She can get jealous but not usually so accusatory," she explains to me before continuing. "I can kind of get her point because he could have asked her to go with him and didn't. Other than that, I don't see much of a problem. Obviously, nothing happened."

I know Julia lost friends in the past over disagreements and that she has no filter, but I don't think that she had always been like this. I wonder what happened to her to make her so distrustful and paranoid.

"Well..." I say, letting my words trail off as I give Kent a look that says "at least I don't act like that."

"So," I ask Yasmin, "see anything interesting on your trip?"

"We found an actual graveyard. Randomly. Practically in the middle of nowhere," she responds.

"Yeah, because an unmarked cemetery is exactly what every campground needs," I say with a sarcastic scoff as they laugh.

Then Kent makes a joke of his own when he says, "Well, it looks like we have another hour to kill while we wait for them to get back. Cornhole anyone?"

Kent and Bruce walk toward the camper to grab and set up the cornhole boards. I join them for a couple rounds until I decide to check on the girls.

I walk inside quietly and notice that they are beginning to rouse from their naps. I soon walk outside, the girls in tow, and we hang out and watch the guys continue to play cornhole. The time passes by quickly as we enjoy the silence, while I simultaneously dread the return of Julia and Jacob's bickering. An hour later, and much to our surprise, they finally return in the golf cart as if nothing is awry.

I'm relieved that apparently Jacob was able to prove to Julia that nothing scandalous happened and that they resolved that extremely awkward argument before they returned.

Julia quickly rushes to the oversized chair where Yasmin is sitting, and she manages to squeeze into the chair with her. I watch as Julia begins to nuzzle Yasmin's shoulder and they begin a hushed discussion. They begin to hold hands and smile at one another. I scrunch my eyebrows at them. Weird. Apparently, we are going to all just forget about what happened a few hours ago.

The animosity, accusations, and betrayal are now irrevocably in the past. The heated arguments and sharp words have faded into a quiet tranquility. Never to be remembered and also never again to be discussed. Which is fine by me because harping on it would just ruin the rest of the weekend.

Julia heads inside and is gone only a short while before she emerges again from the camper with groceries in hand. She proceeds to make everyone sandwiches. We all sit and stand around the picnic table, enjoying them and carrying on.

Jacob wipes the crumbs from his hands onto his jeans and says, "All right, let's hit the lake."

Julia rolls her eyes and says, "Don't take the golf cart to the boat launch. We have plans."

"Yeah, no problem. We can take my truck to the launch," Bruce responds to her demand. Jacob and Bruce start walking toward the truck parked mere feet away from us. I look at Kent, who is taking his time getting up from the table. The others wait on him as he walks over to Erin and me to deliver a goodbye kiss to each of us.

"Good luck, Daddy," I say as I motion for Erin to wave. He waves back at her before walking away to join the other two on what is sure to be an unsuccessful fishing endeavor.

At this moment, I envy the brief length of time it took between the men announcing their departure and the time the ignition started. For us and the children, I expect it'll take much longer and require many more steps.

Julia begins to clean up outside, and I go inside with the girls and Yasmin to begin packing a bag for our next adventure. I walk around the camper, locating all the necessities—diapers, sunscreen, baby wipes, snacks, and drinks.

I create a mental checklist of things that need to be accomplished and check them off as I go. Girls fed—check. Diapers changed—check. Everything in the bag—check. Shoes on—check. Sunscreen on their faces—check.

Julia walks into the camper as I complete my checklist. She tucks away the remaining groceries in the pantry and places the few dirty dishes in the sink.

"We're ready," I announce in a singsong voice.

"Great. Let's go," she says as she grabs her sunglasses off the counter.

Chapter Fourteen

Brooke

Then

We all walk to our ride, and Julia takes her spot in the driver's seat, with Rachel and Yasmin joining her in the front. Erin and I climb onto the back bench seat, our backs to the girls in the front seat. I hook and lock one leg into the bar on the side because Julia tends to drive somewhat erratically. Also, that steep hill we will have to traverse will surely knock Erin and me off the back if we don't sit tight.

I'm pleased when Julia turns slightly to ensure that we are fully seated in the back before she presses the pedal to take off. The path that we take through the campground is finally beginning to feel like a familiar route to me. Geography and navigation have never been strong attributes for me, so I have a small sense of pride knowing that I may be able to make it back to our campsite on memory alone if the occasion arises.

I hold Erin tightly against my chest as we travel. The entire way I point out to her the trees, the birds, the lake, and anything else with names worthy of becoming a part of her vocabulary.

Behind me, in the front seat, I hear Yasmin tell Julia, "Let me know when you want to check out that graveyard, and I can show you the way."

"Oh, I know where it is, but thanks," Julia responds quickly in a particularly sarcastic tone.

I avert my eyes to the side and clench my jaw. Yikes, I'm glad I'm sitting in the back and not up front. I continue to stare out behind the golf cart, watching pebbles fly and scatter as the wheels spin them outward, accompanied by a constant fan of dust.

We pass the boat launch, and although I look for the guys, I don't see them. They must be farther out in the lake by now. Soon, we are at the base of the steep hill, and I once again ensure we are safely situated.

We reach the top, but instead of turning along the cliffside, Julia continues straight on. After a moment, the golf cart jerks rather suddenly to the right as we enter what seems to be an overgrown path. Julia slows down as we analyze our surroundings. I turn around toward the front of the golf cart to try to get an idea of where we're going. We are traveling down a narrow trail lined with tall grass and trees. I see something off in the distance, but I'm not sure what it is. I keep my eyes focused on the end of the trail, and as we get closer, I begin to make out what it is. It's a large shooting target.

"Are we driving in a shooting lane on the archery course?" I ask, shocked.

Julia responds without turning around to meet my eyes. "Sure looks that way. Hope nobody decides to come out here, or we'll be a part of their target practice."

I grimace in turn, saying, "Umm, I guess it's good we started where they shoot from instead of starting from where the target is."

As we approach the target at the end of the lane, Julia stops, and we all get off. I assess the rips in the target, the distance from the location we entered from, and the additional paths and number markers indicating other targets.

"Wait, we didn't come in through the archery section? This aisle was just right off the road like this?" I ask Julia.

"Yeah, the archers begin over there in that field. They shoot at the first aisle there and then continue on by foot, walking on these paths to the next target and then the next. They follow the numbered signs and just shoot arrows all day," she explains.

"Kind of sketchy that we were riding just right there on the road, past that small barrier of tall grass," Yasmin says, "and that a stray arrow could just come out and hit us."

"I'd like to have faith in the people who decided to put this here and think that they thought of everything with safety at the forefront, but I'm not so sure. The fact that we could just turn off the road and right onto an active archery path is ridiculous," I say before continuing. "Don't you think they'd at least have some little poles and a chain to keep people out?"

"Maybe they didn't expect crazy campers to go off-roading up here?" Julia says with a laugh.

"Well, despite how unsafe it seems... you guys want to keep going?" she asks Yasmin and me. We all hold each other's stare for a brief period before we all burst into smiles.

Simultaneously, as I say, "Yes," Yasmin says, "You know it."

"Really, it can't be that dangerous if we can just drive in here without a gate or a warning sign posted," I tell them, trying to stifle my nerves and theirs at the same time.

We all begin to take our original places, deciding to continue to follow the number markers and ride through the shooting lanes. At least I'm facing the back, so I can always say something if I see an archer show up, which I doubt will happen since we are driving faster than anyone would be walking through the course.

As we travel through the archery lanes, the surrounding forest is hushed. I notice an opening in the lane ahead, and as if Julia can read my mind, she slows to a stop to look down the suspicious alcove. As she stops the golf cart, we all peer into the darkness. Julia shrugs and says, "If this hole was a little bit bigger, I'd take this golf cart through there."

Yasmin chuckles nervously before saying, "I think I'd rather go to the graveyard than go down there."

Before we start to move again, Julia turns so that she can face both Yasmin and me.

"This may be the worst time to mention this, as if this place didn't seem sketchy enough, but did y'all hear about how a couple of campers went missing a while back?"

My jaw drops. I look at Yasmin, but she doesn't seem surprised by the news.

"Yeah, didn't that happen like right before we came here one time?" Yasmin asks Julia for confirmation.

"Yeah, that's true. We almost didn't come when we found out," Julia says before focusing her attention more toward me. "Some friends were camping here, and they never checked out of their camping spot. When the park police went to remind them that they missed their checkout time, they were nowhere to be found."

"You've got to be kidding me. You're lying. There's no way you guys would come after that."

"You got me," she concedes with a smirk, "but there's some truth to that story. It didn't happen at this campground, but it did happen at another one nearby."

"Did they ever find them?" I ask, hoping she'll truthfully tell me that it was all a big misunderstanding and is now a campfire story that people love to blow out of proportion.

She shakes her head.

"Nope. No clue what happened either. At least, that was the case last time I thought to check back on it."

Yasmin squeaks, a quiver in her voice. "Jeez, Julia. Why did you think to mention that now?" she inquires.

Julia shrugs. "I just remembered, is all. Next stop—graveyard."

Chapter Fifteen

Brooke

Then

It's just like Julia to tell us such a frightening tale to try to scare us. She did that intentionally. Trying to make us feel inferior, making us want to chicken out and change our minds. But no, I won't let her little ghost story spook me and make her feel like she has the upper hand.

When Yasmin and I don't say anything, she realizes her attempt to dominate us has failed, and she continues on as if nothing happened.

"I'll have to see about getting us out of these lanes first," she mumbles up front to herself.

We continue weaving through the paths from one target to the next before we see the main road through a thicket off to the side.

Julia eases us to a standstill and nods toward the main road.

"Think we should keep going, or should we cut through right here instead?" she asks us.

"I say go through right here if you think you can. I'll shield

Erin from stray branches. No telling how far we'll have to go to get out of these lanes," I tell her as I look at Yasmin, who nods in agreement.

Julia turns the steering wheel hard and pushes us forward through the thin wall of vegetation. Luckily, the twigs snap as we pass rather than acting as a slingshot to sting us.

We slowly ease onto the main road, ensuring there are no other vehicles before turning onto the road completely. Shortly after we begin to drive, Julia says to herself, "Yeah, I know where we are."

She drives for a few minutes before she turns off yet again into the wilderness.

"Good thing y'all got these special tires for all this off-roading," Yasmin says with a laugh.

"Yeah, it's impressive how easily we're getting through all of this grass and mud," I agree.

Just then, we come upon a clearing. The grass is tall but not tall enough to stop us from continuing forward. Ahead there is a narrowing of shrubbery, and as we go through it, I'm surprised to see a football field with trimmed grass on the other side. Despite the weathered field goal posts, I imagine this is still used for recreation since the grass appears to be maintained. We cross the field and enter another narrowing to find the graveyard that they mentioned.

The initial tombstones that catch my attention are small and chipped. However, in the distance, I notice what seems to be a relatively recent and polished grave. Julia pulls into what looks to be the center of the graveyard and stops the golf cart.

"Some of these are so old, the tombstones might even be missing. I hope we aren't parked atop anyone's grave," Julia says with a grimace.

"We stopped for a little while earlier today but only to see th
new burial site over there. I was curious since it looks so nev
It is! They buried her last year! Like, why here, of all places?
Yasmin asks excitedly.

Julia cocks an eyebrow at Yasmin but doesn't comment.

"Hmm. There has to be a good reason? Maybe this is a famil
burial plot, or they really loved to coach football," I say as
gesture my thumb back at the football field we just crossed.

Both Yasmin and Julia laugh at my dark humor.

We all hop off the golf cart, with Yasmin assisting Rachel o
the front seat as I jump off the back with Erin in my arms.

"Yeah, I'd definitely like to check these out and see what th
tombstones say. Morbid curiosity, I guess," Julia says.

Julia points at a dilapidated headstone with her foot and say
"I can hardly tell the year that's written on this one."

I walk up behind her, having placed Erin down to explore, an
I squint my eyes. I, too, cannot determine the year. All I ca
make out is that the year starts with the number one. What
do clearly see is a small ant pile nestled against it, and I quickl
tell the girls, "Watch out for ants," even though they're sti
too young to truly heed my warning.

I walk farther away to admire another section of the graveyar
that has similar small headstones in poor shape.

"Hmm. It says 1912 on this one! Wow!" I say as I read th
foreign names and long-ago dates engraved here.

"Yikes. Most of these are from so long ago, nobody probabl
even visits these graves anymore," Yasmin says, coincidentall
verbalizing my thoughts.

"Right," I agree. "I see 1932, 1938, 1924. All these peopl
were buried here in an unmarked graveyard, deep in the middl
of a public campground."

Next to a football field, at that. I lift one eyebrow at the thought.

I stroll to another headstone, this one more recent, before I say to the others, "This one says 1982. Beloved football coach. This way, he'll never miss a game."

"Shut up! Does it, seriously?" Julia asks me as she stares at me in disbelief.

I flash a devious grin and tell her, "Just kidding."

Julia and Yasmin both roll their eyes at me.

A man's voice begins to float in on the breeze, and we all still, trying to determine the direction from which it's coming.

"Is it just me, or does that sound like Jacob?" Julia asks. I pause to listen closely. I can't hear exactly what he is saying, but Julia's right. It does kind of sound like Jacob.

"Huh. It can't be, though. They're out fishing on the lake," I say, a look of confusion still resting on my face.

"We are all turned around in this place. For all we know, the lake is on the other side of those trees." Yasmin tries to reason, gesturing toward a wall of shrubbery we've yet to explore.

"Jacooob!" Julia screams in the direction the voice came from.

We all wait and watch the woods, wondering if our husbands will trample through the forest or if anyone will respond to Julia's call.

Suddenly, I hear crying coming from behind a tall tuft of overgrown grass. I rush to the sound, immediately identifying the shrieks as Erin's. As I come around the corner, I'm relieved to see that she only tumbled into a hole and that she hasn't stumbled into an enormous pile of ants. The relief is short-lived once I realize that the hole is unusually deep and could possibly be an open grave. I scramble into the dirt and hoist her from the hole quickly just as Julia and Yasmin appear, with Rachel slowly following behind them.

"Did your child fall into a legit open grave?" Yasmin asks me.

I look from the hole to her and then back at the hole. It isn't very deep, maybe two or three feet down into the ground. It's not an exact rectangular shape but more rounded at the edges. The dirt doesn't appear freshly dug, as grass has begun to grow from the mounds surrounding the hole. Honestly, it could be a child's grave because it's small. Then again, I can't see why anyone would bury a child here or why anyone would vandalize a grave here in the middle of nowhere in a mostly forgotten cemetery.

So I start to laugh. How silly are we? Surely, it can't be an open grave. Just a hole. So I continue to laugh because the more I think about it, the funnier it is that we all thought it was an open grave. Soon, we're all laughing. Erin's cries come to a halt as she stares at the three women surrounding her, all hysterically laughing rather than fussing over her.

"Could you imagine?" I say to them as I shake my head, all of us quickly forgetting the mysterious source of the voice in the woods.

Chapter Sixteen

Brooke

Now

I'm going to spend lunch getting to know Grace/Susan/Rebeca. Well, technically, during lunch, she seems to just be Rebeca. I'm even going to break my "no communication" rule. I have to. She is so peculiar, and I have to figure out her ever-apparent identity crisis.

I listen to her drone on about hummingbirds, sunflowers, and painting as I inconspicuously ask her questions. As I do, she doesn't give me much attention, only responding briefly before carrying on about her own interests.

"Do you know anyone here named Grace?" I ask her.

"Hmm, doesn't sound familiar," she responds without thinking for very long.

Blah, blah, birdseed, blah, blah. Or at least that's what I hear. Either she is obnoxiously selfish and only wants to talk about the things she cares about, or she's trying to elude my interrogation.

"Susan can be kind of rude, hmm?" I say. More of a statement, but I ask it as a question, hoping she provides an answer.

She furrows her eyebrows but doesn't say anything. I can't decide if she doesn't want to entertain my inquiries, doesn't care, or doesn't understand.

Blah, blah, hummingbirds prefer, blah, blah.

All right, I need to be more direct. I clear my throat to redirect her attention to me, and when she finally completes her sentence, I ask, "How many different personalities do you have?"

She tilts her head questioningly. She starts to say something but then stops and appears to be pondering my question. Finally. Maybe now I can get some answers out of her.

"You know, you're not the first person to ask me that. I never know what I'm supposed to say," she trails off slightly before continuing. "I guess that's why I'm here."

She shrugs and jumps right back into sunflower facts.

I watch her, analyzing her movements while simultaneously reviewing all that I've learned about her today. She must think I'm interested in her babbling, as she continues on. I want to laugh, truly, but I don't want to hurt her feelings. Of course, that's why she's here. She's crazy. We are all crazy. But isn't knowing I'm crazy supposed to mean that I'm not crazy?

"Oh, my favorite part of the day is next!" she says with excitement, pulling me from my downward spiral. I don't ask what's next. I stare at her, waiting for her to explain, which she does quickly. Man, Rebeca loves to talk.

"Painting! Well, and singing too. I'm most excited about getting to paint a new canvas today." No sooner are the words out of her mouth before we are told to finish up our lunches so we can begin.

Staff members enter the room and begin to take our trays,

remove the tables, and set up easels and paint. They direct us to each choose an easel. I wait for Rebeca to sit and then walk clear across the room and sit as far away from her as I can. Rebeca appears to be my least favorite personality so far. Hmm. I can't help but wonder how many more of them I'll meet.

That poofy-haired lady is back again, strolling to the center of the room.

"Everyone, I'll softly play a popular song on repeat as background noise. I'd like you to pay attention while you paint, and at the end of our session, I'd like us to all sing together!" she says with elation, clapping as she finishes her statement.

Shortly after she takes a seat, a familiar tune begins to play from hidden speakers located somewhere in the room. After a second, I recognize what sounds like "This Little Light of Mine."

Right off the bat, peaceful. Yeah, I get it. But I can see this therapy session quickly turning into a torture session if this is played on repeat for hours straight.

Nevertheless, I grab a paintbrush and begin. Initially, I'm listening to the music, swaying my head gently side to side as I paint. I find myself humming, and as soon as I realize it, I stop.

The music continues in the background, but I begin to ignore it as I immerse myself in my painting. I've never been an artsy person. I don't draw, can't paint. I'm really not very crafty at all. I've never painted on a canvas this size, one almost as big as I am, and I find it peaceful. Instead of striving for perfection, I concentrate on the strokes and the twisting of my wrist as I create swirls upon swirls in a flurry of different colors—olive, maroon, navy, and plum, mostly. Dark colors to match the ever-growing darkness inside me.

Eventually, I raise my eyes to assess the progress of the other painters, and they all appear equally mesmerized, as I'm sure I do. Just like mine, their canvases are nearly complete.

A light clap comes from the poofy-haired lady as she begins, "Everyone, you've done so wonderful. I'll give you all another ten minutes to finish up your pieces, and then we'll begin our sing-along."

After the ten minutes pass, the song begins anew. While others sing in unison, I do not. Deep inside me, though, I feel the need to join in, which is completely out of my usual comfort zone. So I begin to hum along, and that's good enough for me.

She claps as the song finishes and walks around to admire everyone's artwork. When she gets to my canvas, she says, "I love the story that this piece tells. Wonderful job."

I smile shyly. Nothing but erratic swirls and circles are on my canvas, so I don't know what she means.

Once she makes her way around the room, she announces to us all, "Individual sessions are next! It was a pleasure working with you all today. Please, make your way to the lobby and wait for your sessions to begin. Have a great day!"

With that, I follow everyone out of the room, and I wait in the lobby with the others. I don't have to wait long before my name is called. I get up from my chair in the waiting room and follow the receptionist, who guides me to an office down the hall.

We approach an open door, and the orderly motions with her hand toward the door. Ugh, therapy. Not my thing.

As I approach, a wave of unease and dread suddenly flushes my system. When I attempt to cross the threshold, I freeze. It feels as if I can't move. My hand trembles softly, similar to the motion when one tries to force the opposite ends of a magnet together. I have to push forward with considerable effort to pass through the deflective force. I walk through the open door and into a small room that smells of teakwood.

Sitting across the room, in a plush red chair, poised confidently and wearing an enigmatic smirk, is my new shrink.

Chapter Seventeen

Brooke

Then

After our graveyard adventure, we ended up back at the camper before the sun even had a chance to set. It was still too early to try to put the girls down for the night, so instead we decided to enjoy the lower temperatures that come with the setting sun, and we're now playing with the girls outside the camper.

Shortly after the light of the day begins to fade from view completely, our husbands get back from their fishing trip. I grab my phone from my pocket to check the time, only to realize that I left it inside since it's useless without any service.

Each of our husbands hop out of the truck, walking to their respective wives, no doubt to tell us about all the fish they didn't catch. Kent walks toward me, placing a kiss atop Erin's head before asking me how our day was. I fervently describe our adventures from the day, everything from cruising through archery lanes to graveyard diving. He laughs when I tell him how scared I was that Erin fell into an open grave. His laughter gets everyone's attention, and he begs me to tell everyone what happened, and sure enough, they all break out into fits of laughter with the retelling of my story.

"Man, we tried to fish all day and didn't catch anything," he tells me.

I notice specifically how he says they didn't catch a fish rather than didn't get any bites. Semantics at its finest. They do this at home too. The guys—or at least Kent and Jacob—find any excuse not to stay at home. They don't want to change dirty diapers, be responsible for the kids, and be expected to do chores around the house. And so they make themselves scarce. They can often be found outside, busying themselves with tasks that appear semi-important so that they can escape duties without consequence.

Just as we get the pleasantries out of the way, a cacophony of high-pitched buzzing begins to descend upon us. The cicadas hum in their intense-yet-rhythmic tone, signaling that the dim light of the sun will soon be eradicated by the darkness that the night brings.

We rush inside to eat supper, evading the pesky bugs that emerge in hordes as soon as the shadows of the night begin to settle into finality.

As we get inside, Julia tells Jacob, "You know, we could have sworn we heard you earlier today while we were in the graveyard."

Jacob looks at her, perplexed.

"I'm pretty sure that the graveyard isn't that close to the lake. Wasn't me. I mean, I did yell at one point when I got a bite on the line. I was rubbing it in these losers' faces too," he says, gesturing his thumb toward Kent and Bruce. "But even with all that, I don't think y'all could have heard me from where y'all were."

I ponder this and begin to rationalize. Julia had just told us that eerie story. We likely heard some other weekend camper and gave Julia the benefit of the doubt that it was Jacob to subconsciously ease our fear of a stranger lurking in the woods.

No one speaks as we begin to get things ready for supper. I'm sure we girls are each in our thoughts about what happened earlier.

The room remains quiet as we all eat supper inside. The light hum of the music plays outside, breaking what would be awkward silence without it. I guess I'll speak up to liven the mood.

"Who wants to lose to me and Kent in Pedro tonight?" I ask the group.

Jacob boos at me from across the room.

"You sure talk a lot of shit for someone who just learned how to play," he says to me, lifting an eyebrow in accusation.

"Someone must feel intimidated," I suggest to him while tilting my head to the side.

"She does have that horseshoe stuck up her ass. She might lose here and there, but she wins more than she should," my husband says, shaking his head.

I roll my eyes and say, "Jealous," before sticking out my tongue.

"Before we play Pedro, we need to get these kids to bed first. Let's give them a bath together," Julia says, looking at me.

I grab a paper towel to remove the crumbs off Erin's hands and throw away our plates before walking across the camper to join Julia at the tub, which she already has running. I place Erin down next to Rachel, and we clean off today's shenanigans from their hair and skin.

We dry off the girls and tell them to give each other a kiss good night. Julia stays in her room to put Rachel to sleep, and I set off across the camper to our room, stopping to let Kent kiss Erin good night.

"We'll play a round while y'all put the kids to bed," he tells me, and I nod in agreement.

I lie down in my bed with Erin, letting her pinch my arm fat as she falls asleep. Every now and then, she stirs when she hears the others get rambunctious outside the door, but she is so tired that her eyes stay closed. It's not long before I can slip out of her grasp and leave the room. I kiss her forehead before easing back out to join the others.

I walk out to see that Julia was unsuccessful at putting Rachel to bed, as I spot her on the sofa watching a video on her tablet.

"No luck?" I ask Julia, nodding to Rachel.

"Not a chance. I'll let her stay up for a little longer and then try again," she explains to me.

Julia and I sit near the table and watch Jacob and Kent face off against Yasmin and Bruce in a game of cards.

Jacob loudly lets out a string of profanities when he loses a round, and I still myself, listening to determine if it woke Erin, but no sound comes from our room. They play another round before Kent and Jacob win the game. Yasmin and Bruce exit their seats as Julia and I replace them, and Kent and Jacob grab another round of beers.

Yasmin goes to sit on the sofa, a novel in her hand, and Bruce joins them, watching us begin our card game.

I laugh at myself as we begin, as I still don't fully understand this game. I do love games, though, and luckily I'm no sore loser or bad winner. I'm content to just play for the heck of it. Julia is competitive, though, and I see it blatantly as we play, with her intermittently bashing our choices and mocking the moves that we make.

"Rachel's finally falling asleep over there," Julia says, pointing her chin to the sofa, where Rachel sits between Yasmin and Bruce.

"I'll go lie down with her," Yasmin says, placing her bookmark between the pages and closing it.

Julia nods in thanks as Yasmin walks past us to go lie down in the main room with Rachel.

Kent and I lose the first game. I shrug in defeat as Julia scratches out our names on the score sheet and replaces it with *Losers*.

"Another round?" Julia asks the table, and we all nod in agreement. We continue like that for the next hour—playing, goading one another, drinking, and laughing while the smell of beer wafts through the air alongside the reverberation of vulgar language.

Yasmin sneaks out of the room right before we are about to lose again, softly closing the door behind her, tiptoeing toward us. She sits down on the sofa and asks, "Who's winning?"

"Who do you think?" Julia asks with a chuckle.

Yasmin surprises me when she says, "Brooke. That girl is smart."

I blush but not for long because, of course, Julia's remark serves as an insult when she says, "Book smart, maybe. But that's it."

Julia doesn't laugh. She doesn't even wink. Julia is like that though—direct and unapologetic in all things. She's hard to understand sometimes. I never take it personally, and I always let it roll off my shoulders. My mom always told me that when people are mean that they're just jealous, and even now as an adult, I can see her insight wasn't far off the mark.

Once again, we lose the game, but I don't focus on it too much.

"Yasmin and Bruce, play me and Kent?" Jacob asks the couple sitting on the couch.

"Umm, no. How is that fair? It should always be the same partners. You guys can't switch it up whenever you feel like it," Julia cries.

I wave a hand in the air and tell Julia, "I don't care. It's a four-person game, and there's six of us. This way, we make sure everyone gets a chance to play."

"I care," she says, lifting an eyebrow. "I won, so I should be able to play again."

I look around the room to find everyone averting their eyes and no one attempting to speak for or against her.

"Never mind," she says. "You guys play. Brooke and I are going to take advantage of our kid-free time. We're going make wind," she tells the room.

I lift my eyebrows in confusion before voicing my concern, "Can we go out on the golf cart this late at night?"

"I don't see why not. Yasmin, are you coming for a ride?" she asks her friend.

"In the woods? At night? Alone? No thanks, I'll stay here," she replies.

"We won't be alone. We'll be together." She attempts to rationalize with Yasmin.

Yasmin's jaw starts to quiver slightly before she says, "I think it might rain later. I'm seriously too afraid to go out there in the dark and the rain. Besides, they need four to play cards. You guys are good. Y'all go! We'll hang back and keep an eye on the girls."

Julia doesn't argue with her as she proceeds to get up from the table and put her shoes on. I follow her lead. I don't mind going with her, even though she really didn't give me a choice. It's not like I can hang back and play on my phone. I also can't understand why Yasmin would be scared. Perhaps she has seen too many horror movies, or may be currently engrossed in a creepy book, or may still be frightened from Julia's story earlier today.

I give Kent a kiss as I pass him and say, "Shouldn't be long. Y'all have fun."

I follow Julia down the camper stairs, noticing that she didn't tell Jacob goodbye, which isn't peculiar, seeing as how they hardly talk anyway. Julia gets behind the wheel, as always, and we make our way onto the road. She drives slowly, although I'm not sure if it's because she's nervous about driving at night, or if it's because she's having trouble seeing the road without the constant glow of street lamps.

"Hope you don't mind coming for a ride. I mean, what else could we do?" she asks me as she drives past the boat launch.

A thought crosses my mind at her statement, and I ask, "You have your phone?"

"No," she replies, "it's back at the camper, but we shouldn't need it. You have yours?"

"Nah, my service sucks over here," I tell her.

"That's because you have a stupid android," she tells me.

I roll my eyes. I always get comments like this from her, and I don't get it. My android works just fine, if not better than her phone. It's my cell phone provider that sucks, but there's no point in trying to argue with her.

As we reach the base of the hill, a bright cluster of lightning illuminates the sky in the distance. Julia brings the golf cart to a stop as we watch the sky. I wait for the sound of thunder to follow, but it never does. The giant light show continues intermittently, overpowering the dark sky. Heat lightning, it must be, rages wild like a fire far away from the lake, briefly illuminating the darkness as it crescendos. The lightning dances erratically, washing us not with rain but instead an ominous cloud of unease.

"How peculiar to see lightning and hear no thunder," I say breathlessly, not taking my eyes away from the beautiful and chaotic monstrosity.

"Good thing Yasmin didn't come, because that shit's creepy," Julia says before beginning our ascent up the steep hill.

Chapter Eighteen

Brooke

Now

Soon after entering this man's office, I sat on a cushioned love seat across from him, and I have averted my eyes since. Even now, as the clock ticks echo through bouts of silence, I continue to look down at the floor after he introduces himself and peppers me with conversational remarks between islands of silence. I notice that he doesn't ask many questions. He makes a lot of general statements. He pauses between each statement, allowing me ample time to respond. Ha, yeah, good luck with that. I feel like this is a strategy that he uses with people like me, and I'm not going to fall for it.

He introduced himself as my psychiatrist after I sat down, but I was distracted. Too focused on cataloging him, judging and assessing his physical attributes and character. He smells like any other guy and also looks like your stereotypical therapist—semi-stocky, slightly handsome, average height, full head of brown hair, and a pair of eyeglasses perched upon his nose. Out of the corner of my eye, I see him looming, his legs crossed and a notepad in hand.

He can try to talk to me all he wants. I don't talk to many people, and something about him has my entire mind and body on the defensive. It's not like I can read people, or decipher auras, or that I'm even a good judge of character. I typically see people as plain old good people until their actions prove otherwise. Or at least I did, back when things were normal and before my life changed forever.

This is such a peculiar situation that I have found myself in. I don't know how to explain the cloud of unease I feel in this room with him. And I have to work one-on-one with him for the duration of this program? I cannot comprehend how I will endure it. He will want me to talk, and that's what I don't do—talk. I fear I may not have the strength to share things with him, but that's not atypical for me.

What if they remove me from the day program for lack of participation? Oh no no no. This program has just begun, and who knows what else I can get out of this experience.

I take a deep breath in an effort to banish this ominous feeling and these speculative thoughts. Truly, I'm being ridiculous. He's just a man who wants to hear what I have to say. Well, there's the problem. I don't ever want to say anything. That's what it all comes down to, and that's why I don't particularly care for him.

The man—I think he called himself Dr. G—notices my efforts and identifies the intention behind my technique. He must be able to tell I'm trying to calm my nerves and center myself. Or, at least if he's a good shrink, he should be able to.

"You're safe here," he tells me calmly.

I flinch at his remark. How does something that was surely meant to reassure me make me cower in fear? I find his voice unsettling.

"I understand that I'm a new face and you may not wish to talk just yet," he says to me. I drop my shoulders in relief. "But I do hope to receive more communication from you as our interactions persist."

"Ultimately, I'd like to discuss the night that you lost your friend and the details surrounding that horrible tragedy," he says, pausing for a while before he speaks again.

I hate that he pauses, because in the silence, there's no way to redirect my mind, no way to keep it from flashing vivid images from that night, rapidly one after the other, building into a wave of terror. His words disturb the facade I've built up. His voice triggers me, causing details of that night to enter my consciousness.

Playing cards.

Lightning.

Trees.

Mud.

A knife.

Blood.

Darkness.

A tear rolls down my cheek, prompting Dr. G to speak again as he tells me, "We will not rush there. All in due time, of course. Actually, we can talk about anything you'd like."

See. This. I don't like this. I don't want to remember. I don't want to relive it. I want to accept my punishment and coast through life, trying to vanquish the memories as I waste away in the shell of my body.

I need to talk. I know I do. I know it can't hurt me—at least it can't physically. I'm already as bad off as it can get. What is worse than this fate, this one that I have already endured for so

long? I should talk. I can say anything, really. I will. One day.
I can only hope that the right person is there to listen.

Chapter Nineteen

Brooke

Then

We reach the top of the hill, and just like the first time we came here, we venture off the main path and along the cliff that rests around the lake.

Yikes, it's even scarier now that it's dark. An irrational fear comes to mind and sinks its claws in deep. Maybe at some point today, the dirt crumbled and a portion of this path fell down the cliffside into the lake. We wouldn't know. Wouldn't even be able to see the hole in the ground before it was too late. The golf cart would nosedive and fall to the side, careening farther down into the lake. Would the fall kill us first, or would we drown, trapped in the mangled golf cart?

I shake my head, attempting to remove the thought from my head. I try to reassure myself, thinking back to the path the last time I saw it, in the daylight. Surely there was enough room between the cliff's edge and the path we now travel on. Not to mention someone would have noticed the cliff crumbling into the lake and cordoned off this area, if that were the case.

I sigh with relief as I successfully dispel the anxiety I have caused myself.

"You know what I just thought of?" I laugh aloud. "How crazy it would be to not realize that a section of this path was missing and us falling to our deaths because of it, unaware," I explain to her in an attempt to further confirm my fear as irrational.

"I can see that. We could lose traction, and the golf cart would go over the edge. I'd have better luck getting out because I'm closer to the trees. I could grab one and save myself," Julia says before continuing. "But you're on the edge. You'd go down. And they'd all be sitting back at the camp waiting for us, oblivious to the whole thing. It would take me a while to walk back to them without the golf cart. I probably wouldn't get back until morning."

I'm not sure if she's mocking me, being facetious, or truly going down a similar rabbit hole like I just did, so I contribute to her vivid depiction of an alternate reality.

"Yeah," I say, "or campers would see the golf cart go down with someone inside, and everyone would start raising the alarm and trying to find me in the water. They'd hear all the commotion, and they'd know one of us was likely dead, but not which one of us until you'd reach them."

We both stare at each other before bursting into a fit of laughter.

I gasp and tell her, "Oh my god, we should write a book."

"Absolutely," Julia agrees. "I'm writing that down in my notes before we leave."

She steers us into the woods and away from the cliff's edge, and again, I breathe a sigh of relief, knowing that we won't be falling off the cliff.

Julia slows the golf cart down as we enter the dark woods, as there is less light here, the dim moonlight unable to penetrate the canopy of the trees.

Suddenly, someone in the bushes grabs me, and I scream, throwing myself toward Julia, trying to escape whoever's assaulting me. Instead of racing away from my attacker, she slows the golf cart to a stop completely.

"What was that?" she shouts at me as she turns back to look at where we just were. I turn, too, quickly identifying the perpetrator.

A bare branch juts out from the bushes, hovering above the path.

"That branch scared the shit out of me," I explain to Julia.

"The branch? The way you screamed, I thought there was maybe a spider or a man in the woods," Julia says, shaking her head.

"Fuck," Julia whispers.

I follow her gaze and notice a tent and a campfire in the distance.

"Well, maybe your loud-ass scream didn't wake them up. The fire's lit, so at least they're still awake."

I continue staring at the tent, but I don't see anyone sitting around the fire. I purse my lips, hoping that we don't end up disturbing them. We aren't that close to them, but when I screamed, I know they must have heard me.

She doesn't continue driving, though, instead stilling us. I look around and quickly notice that we're near the picturesque frame of the lake.

"Guess they're camping primitive tonight. We should really try that one day," Julia comments.

"I'd love to one day. I used to go camping in Girl Scouts, and that was always the most fun," I inform Julia.

She twists her lips.

"I didn't know you were in Girl Scouts." She pauses before snorting out a small laugh. "Too bad they couldn't teach you deductive reasoning skills while you were there."

I'm happy I'm not facing her when she says that because I feel rage dance across my face. Until now, I've dealt with the un-filtered comments and snide remarks with grace, ignoring her and refusing to acknowledge them. Apparently, my methods aren't working, so I guess I'll have to modify my reactions.

I turn to her and offer her my most-menacing smile as I tell her, "Oh, there's a lot you don't know about me."

I think my intention to intimidate her works to an extent because she begins to backpedal, which she doesn't usually do.

"You're book smart, you know, and so nice, but you don't always pick up on things." She laughs, an attempt to disarm me.

"How do you say that? *Wolf in sheep's clothing.*" I offer her with a wink.

She laughs again before shushing me and gesturing toward some movement around the fire.

We sit and watch. Stalking these innocent people. I hope they heard us driving and that we haven't totally spooked them. I can only barely make out one figure sitting near the fire, and it appears that he has his back turned to us. We don't move. I think Julia is unsure of which direction to go, given there are inhabitants nearby that we may be disturbing.

I look up through a small hole in the canopy of the trees above, and I see the stars, far brighter than I am used to seeing them back at home. There's so much less light pollution here, and the stars are mesmerizing. I wish I had noticed sooner. I'm so used to viewing the night sky and hardly seeing anything through the fog and artificial light clusters. Until now, I forgot to observe them here, away from all the barriers that we have at home. Taking in the stars fills me with awe, as it's a luxury I won't have once we return home. I'll have to keep Erin up a little longer than I usually do tomorrow and bring her outside to watch the stars perform for us.

I see something move out of the corner of my eye. I turn my head to find the man getting up from the fire and disappearing into the shadows.

"Guess we'll stay here for a few minutes and then cruise through and come out of the other side?" she whispers, asking for my approval.

I nod and then motion for her to look up and enjoy the view.

Chapter Twenty

Brooke

Then

We're both sitting still, looking up at the night sky, when Julia suddenly falls off the cart. No, someone is pulling her off with force. Thanks to the dim light cast by the thousands of stars shining above us, I can make out the form of a man. It appears that he's young—a kid, really—and he's yanking her from her seat with little effort on his part. He has taken us both by surprise, but especially Julia, as she's stunned, eyes wide, being thrown to the ground. He isn't trying to hide his face, but it doesn't matter because I don't recognize him.

What the hell is even happening? Is he going to hurt us? We weren't even doing anything. It's possible that he's upset that we interrupted his quiet time, but this is the most inappropriate way to handle the situation.

No, this can't be real. He's going to hurt Julia. *Julia.* I'm frozen. I don't know what to do. Even if I did know what to do, I don't think I'd be able to move. I'm so scared right now. He'll probably just hurt me if I try to help. I can't run either. Surely, he'll chase me down to ensure I can't escape.

Just then, Julia begins to push herself up from the ground. She's better than me, trying to defend herself. Meanwhile, I can only watch it all unfold. I'm trying to be optimistic. I'm positive that he'll realize his error and apologize, letting us go. After all, we haven't done anything to deserve this. That is what I continue to hope until he steps on her, holding her down.

Even though his foot is on her back and she can't lift herself, she still tries to break free from him. As she begins to lift herself from the ground, the man bends down and grabs her by the shoulders, aggressively trying to lift her, but Julia fights back. She squirms from his grasp, trying to escape.

The man stands up and steps back, and just as I think he's going to let her get up and let us go, he kicks her shoulders, making her roll onto her back. He bends down again, grabbing her shoulders to lift her from the ground, but she pulls away. Then he grabs her by the neck, tightening his hands, choking her as he yanks her up from the ground.

He stands there, staring into her eyes as her fight diminishes and her body weakens under his grip. Once he realizes that he has taken the fight from her, he lets her weak and sagging body crash back to the ground.

He then falls to the ground after her, and on his knees beside her, he makes a swift movement in the air before bringing his arm down forcefully to stab her. I silently plead that he'll stop, that once he sees the blood, he'll repent. Instead, he reignites my fear as he lifts his arm again to stab her once more.

A scream erupts from me.

No, no, no! Why'd I do that? He's looking at me now and away from the bloody body beneath him. Shit, how can I be so selfish and self-preserving at a time like this?

I begin to will my body to move. I have to get out of here. *Fuck. Fuck. Fuck.*

I'm shuffling off the seat, clumsy and unsteady, as my legs are gelatin beneath me. Unable to follow the commands my brain is sending them. I struggle to plant myself on the ground, all the while smelling a hint of blood floating on the breeze.

Which way should I even run? I turn again quickly to see how close he is to capturing me, and instead, my eyes focus on something behind him. In the distance, I see a man's head.

Help! Help is here.

Oh, thank god. I begin to yell at the man, screaming so loud that my voice cracks as I do. I wave my hands, just in case, making sure he'll be able to get to us as quickly as possible.

"Help!"

The killer seems frozen by the other man's appearance, just as I was frozen when he began assaulting Julia.

Good. Fuck him and his psycho ass. Just as the other man begins to run toward us, heavy rainfall pours from the sky above. Sheets of rain crash down upon us, impairing my ability to see clearly.

The other man comes crashing through the shrubbery, taking a moment to analyze the scene before him. His brow furrows as he tries to peer through the rain to determine what's happening.

Well, shit. I can help.

"H-h-h-he killed Julia!" I stammer before continuing. "We haven't done anything, I swear. We were just passing by, and he attacked us!"

"Is that true?" he asks the younger man.

Yes, it's fucking true. He's literally on top of her, covered in her blood, with a knife in his hand. I know it's raining, but obviously, the second man has got to see what's going on.

Lightning strikes then, illuminating the gruesome scene around us. The thunder roars soon afterward, almost as if vocalizing disbelief at the atrocities inflicted by the young man near me.

He then looks down at what he's done, as if he, too, heard the personification of the thunderous onslaught. I watch his face, and I can so clearly see what he's feeling. Remorse, I think. Not remorse for what he's done but remorse he wasn't able to kill us both before getting caught.

The older man looks at me, an outstretched hand beckoning me toward him, and asks, "You watched him do this to her?"

I run to him, around Julia's body, far from the monster's reach so that he can't pull me in as I try to reach safety. When I reach the second man, I quickly turn to face the killer, ensuring that he cannot sneak up behind me and attempt to stab me while my back is turned.

"Yes." I nod. "We stopped right here to look at the stars, and he just came out of nowhere and started hurting her! He started choking her, and then... then..." That's when sobs start to escape from me. I try to speak but can hardly get air in, let alone formulate sentences to explain what happened.

Oh no, the baby. Julia's poor unborn child. I clench my eyes shut, unable to keep the tears at bay any longer.

Suddenly, my head falls forward as something heavy slams into it from behind. The pain is horrible, and a warm sensation is spreading from my scalp down my neck. I try to turn my head, but I can't, as I'm suddenly overcome with pain, unable to move without making it worse. I see a large rock from the corner of my eye, and I'm unable to defend myself as it comes crashing down on me.

* * *

I awake, my entire body stiff. I'm so cold and soaking wet, and my skin feels filthy. I try to open my eyes, but it's difficult. That's when I hear mumbling. I still my breathing, keep my eyes closed, and try to listen. I think I detect voices, but they seem muffled. I strain to hear over the sound of my thundering heartbeat.

"Don't you get it? Don't you... why I did what... did?" I hear someone say, some of the words inaudible. There's a pause before the same voice continues. "Probably not. You only see me for all... faults."

Another voice, a stronger, deeper one, speaks next.

"You've got to understand..."

There's a long pause, with no one speaking. Or if they are, I can't hear them.

"What?" the softer voice asks.

I'm trying so hard to listen, hoping they'll go away before they realize I'm still alive. But then dirt begins to fall on top of me in large deposits. I'm going to die here. No one will rescue me. They may find me, but it'll be too late. As the pressure increases atop my body, all I can think about is how my family will have to exist without me in it.

II

Part Two

Chapter Twenty-One

CJ

Then

Thank god this awful fishing trip appears to be coming to an end when Dad yawns and looks at me, asking, "Ready to head in, bud?"

I nod, and he proceeds to steer the boat back to the shore. It doesn't take long, and soon we are coasting up onto the bank, the water rippling out in small waves behind us. I hop out, and Dad follows behind me as we exit the boat, leaving everything in the boat on the bank.

"Oh, let me get our phones," he says, turning around to retrieve them from the small boat.

I follow him as he walks back to our site, red-brown dust fanning out beneath his heavy footfalls with every step. It's still empty here at the moment, with no other campers in sight.

"We should set up our home for the night," he suggests as we walk up the steep bank.

He throws our phones down on our ice chest once we get back to the truck.

I don't argue with him as we unload our bags and I start to help him assemble our makeshift house. He gets frustrated as we go about it, as he's rusty and it's obvious he hasn't set this tent up in a while. Even though I'm actively helping him and offering advice, he snaps at me throughout the whole process. *Excuse me, would you rather I watch you do the whole thing yourself?* I only think about it because saying it aloud will only make things worse.

Finally, the further along we get into the process, the easier it is, and soon it's set up and sturdy. Dad shakes it for good measure, and it hardly budges.

He chuckles lightly as he says, "Well, son, I'll be honest. I had ulterior motives. I think I'm going to test this bad boy out and take a nap."

A moment of silence passes between us until I break it and say, "I'll just chill out here."

"Suit yourself. Maybe we can go walk around these woods later or go fishing again," he tells me before retiring inside the tent.

I grab my phone to occupy myself, but I also listen to the rustling inside the tent while I scroll on it. Luckily, only minutes pass before I hear him start to snore. Now's my chance to see why Mom was texting him. I lift his phone, and as I swipe my finger over the screen, I'm happy to see that he doesn't have a passcode set up. The home screen comes alive, and I notice the number one on the messaging app, indicating Dad hasn't read the message yet.

Oh, well. I'm reading it because something isn't sitting right with me.

I open up the messaging app and choose the conversation between my mom and my dad. The most recent text says, *Does he seem to suspect anything?*

What the fuck does that mean? I scroll and start to read messages from earlier this month.

Mom: *His behavior is out of control.*

Dad: *Yes, with me too.*

Mom: *I don't know what to do.*

Dad: *I have an idea. Hold up. Let me send you the link.*

Dad: *behavioraloutreachfacility.com*

Mom: *Absolutely. That's what we should do. Call me later tonight, and we can discuss signing him up.*

Dad: *He won't like it, but he's done it to himself. Call you later.*

The thread for that conversation ends, and the next conversation seems to be from earlier this week.

Dad: *Okay, they accepted him. He starts Monday. Come over to the house Friday around 3 to tell him goodbye, but don't say anything. The last thing I need is for him to realize I'm dropping him off after the trip.*

Mom: *Does he suspect anything?*

What the actual fuck? I click the link from the text messages. It brings me to a website for military schools. I read the home page.

Is your young adult, between the ages of sixteen and eighteen years old, testing boundaries, acting out, and/or defiant to parents and figures of authority? You've found the right place! We offer a network of programs that are geared toward transitioning your defiant young adult into a functioning member of society! Our methods are militant and strict, as we emphasize discipline and obedience. Our programs are located throughout the United States. Would you like to know more? Please enter your email below, and we will contact you within one to three business days with information on our programs as well as locations available in your area.

You have got to be kidding me! They're sending me to military school? I turn and listen again to ensure that snoring is still coming from inside. Once I confirm he's still asleep, I begin to remove any evidence that I made this discovery. I delete the Internet tab that was opened by the link that I clicked, and I also mark the text message as unread.

I sit there in silence, staring out at the water. So they've really just given up on me? They're going to make me someone else's problem. I can't believe them, and I can't believe I couldn't even tell anything was going on. I should have known.

I stomp off, crushing leaves below my feet and punching branches out of my way as I walk. Fuck this, and fuck them if they think they can get one over on me. I storm off to explore without Dad. I don't even care what he'll say when he wakes up and sees that I'm gone. My feet kick up dust as I slam them into the dirt. I need time to think, time to plan, and time to figure out how I'm going to handle this. But mostly, I'm so pissed that I need to go and find a way to blow off some steam.

* * *

I keep walking. Walking out of the gate, down the road, and going down and up hills. I walk so much that I make it down into the campground that surrounds the lake. I walk past the boat launch, and that's when I decide I'll walk around the campers. Although I've cooled down a bit, I still have some steam to blow off.

Maybe I'll people watch and eavesdrop a little here and there.

As I walk the gravel path, I see a few older couples sitting outside in dead silence. I see plenty of groups of college kids drinking and getting loud. A good chunk of the campers that I watch are young families with their kids. As I walk, almost all the dogs that I encounter either bark at me or try to chase me down.

Wait a minute. There's a golf cart coming down the road, and it sure does look familiar. There's no way I could ignore that neon-yellow thing, even if I tried. I see some of the women from earlier nearby, so I bet that's where it's about to pull in. I quickly duck and vanish behind a nearby camper, which appears to be unoccupied. I'm hidden from their view, close enough that I can hear bits of their conversation. Occasionally, I peek around the corner to watch them.

I feel rushed, and I'm curious if Dad has woken up yet. I want to be back before he wakes up so that I don't make him angry. I don't want to hang around long, but I can't help my curiosity. The women were pretty hot, and I want to see who they're with.

They all seem to have boyfriends, or at least I can tell that they seem to have an equal guy-girl ratio. The kids aren't outside, so I'm unsure as to who they belong to. That one woman is still being a bitch, I confirm, because I hear her bickering. "—can't stay here with me and your child?"

I catch a portion of what the nagging woman says. I'm actually confused as to how she has so many friends because this is only the second time that I've seen her and she seems to always be saying something negative to those around her.

I then get a text from Dad, asking where I am, which makes me quickly scurry away, back toward our campsite at the base of the hill.

I text him back and tell him I'm on my way back to the tent.

I'm surprised that he doesn't say he's mad. Instead, all his reply says is: *Okay, waiting on you.*

Chapter Twenty-Two

CJ

Then

I find myself hidden in the woods, sitting down on a broken log, finally having calmed down after the ultimate betrayal by my parents that I discovered earlier today. It wasn't easy to stop seething. I walked for a good long time before I finally wound up here. I haven't made it back to the primitive camping sites yet, but I'm pretty sure I'm close.

When my dad texted me earlier, I tried to hurry back because I knew that my absence was likely to upset him. He woke up and saw I wasn't there, and he knows I'm on my way back. Doesn't matter how fast I am. I'm sure he'll be upset that I wasn't there when he woke up. I started to slow down the moment it clicked, when I realized I didn't have to keep rushing because I was already in trouble, regardless.

I found some trails off the main path, and I've been exploring, but I got a little tired and decided to rest. I don't feel like I've wandered too far or that I'm lost. This place can't really be that big. I'm sure if I keep following the trails, eventually I'll see something familiar that'll send me back in the right direction.

It's pretty quiet out here. I hear a bird off in the distance, and a lot of bugs buzz by to land atop my sweat-dampened skin, but I only brush them off as they do. Just as I'm about to rise from the sturdy log, I detect a rumbling sound in the distance. I still my movements and duck my head, directing my gaze toward it. Soon, I identify the source of the sound. A golf cart emerges from another path, across a small clearing ahead of me. Not just any golf cart either. That same yellow one, I'm sure of it.

I crawl off the log and onto the firm ground, hoping they'll pass me and go about their business without trying to speak to me. Unfortunately, the golf cart stops. I think they're about ten yards away. I don't know. I've never been good at math.

I look at the man and woman, and sure enough, it's a couple from that group I spied on earlier today.

They're talking, but they're whispering, which is ridiculous because there's no one around to hear them. Or at least, that's what they should be thinking as I stay here, hidden in the bushes. I can't get up now. It'll be so awkward, and I might spook them.

Their whispers turn to giggles, and I adjust my vision to focus on them more. They're still seated in the golf cart, which I'm thankful for as I'd hate for them to get out and walk around, only to find me crouching in the bushes, intentionally hiding from them.

I squint my eyes to adjust my vision, and I gape at the scene unfolding before me. My man! He's slipping his hand up her skirt. They seriously sneaked off to mess around. I've got to give them props. They're probably sharing a camper with their family and kids and don't want to make too much noise in their camper with all their guests. But out here, deep in the woods, no one can see or hear them. Except me, of course.

I can't tear my eyes away from them as I sit crouched in the bushes, watching them go at it. It's like my own personal movie. I watch them perform for me. They're doing all the foreplay, just like I've seen before in the videos I search for online. She's beautiful, her long hair falling to frame her face. I hear my heartbeat accelerate, and I wince even though I know they can't hear the thrumming as loud as I do.

The woman stops for a moment and looks around quickly to make sure no one is watching them. She must be so hungry for him that her vision blurs because she still doesn't catch sight of me. They continue on, and I enjoy watching the whole thing unfold in front of me. I even take out my phone and record some of the good parts.

Eventually, they finish their assignation and end it with a sensual kiss. Once they appear to have finished, they straighten their shirts, sit up tall, and do a visual scan to ensure they left no evidence of their romantic tryst behind. Their laughter radiates through the clearing as they lock eyes with one another. Shortly after that, they leave, heading back the way they came and leaving a cloud of dust in their wake.

One would think after the free show that I just got that I'd be jovial and spritely, but instead, I'm the opposite. While I can't deny how devious and thrilled I am, I'm also, once again, left alone with my thoughts.

I drop my head into my hands as the anger I felt earlier renews. My euphoria is quickly replaced with malice. What I just experienced was living, and my parents want to take that away from me.

Chapter Twenty-Three

CJ

Then

After they leave, I pull out my phone and send a text to my dad

Me: *Think I got a little lost, but I finally recognize where I am. Be back soon.*

Dad's reply shows up almost immediately.

Dad: *I was about to hop in the truck and go look for you. I still can if you need me to?*
   Me: *Nah, I got it*

I have a hard time believing that he finally decided to start worrying about me. I think he's just afraid of losing sight of me when he's so close to getting rid of me. His texts sound like he's concerned, and he may be, but he isn't concerned about my safety. He's concerned I'll run away before he gets the opportunity to mold me into a good little servant at tha military school.

I'm still in no rush to get back to camp because, seriously, what's he going to do about it? He's already abandoning me, which is the worst thing that he could do.

My emotions sputter like a malfunctioning radiator. I get mad, cool down, and just go and get mad again. I keep thinking, and I still can't decide what to do.

Do I let them send me away, try to reform myself, and become the child of their dreams? Do I run away now before they have the chance to send me off? Do I go to the camp, gather a few things, and then run away from there once he falls asleep? Or do I go to that school, wait it out, and return home as the same person who left? Surprise, motherfucker! Can't get rid of me that easily.

Just as I'm about to lift myself from the ground, a familiar sound begins to echo through the trees. I glance up in the same direction as earlier, and sure enough, that neon-yellow golf cart appears once again. I shake my head in disbelief. These two are insatiable. I duck again and watch the golf cart pull into the same spot as earlier, but this time, the man is accompanied by a different woman.

Hmm, I can't help but wonder what they're doing here and what their relationship is. I don't have to wait long, though, as their conversation begins, and the woman is loud enough for me to hear everything she says.

"You came here?" she asks, looking at him with accusation and disbelief.

"Yeah, once we came into the clearing, there were some rabbits. We stopped because Yasmin told me she wanted to see them," he explains to her.

"Did you see bears too? Lions, even? Because you guys were

here a lot longer than a fleeting bunny-watching session," she retorts.

"Julia, we still have a few more stops. Chill out. I can't believe you. I'm going to show you everywhere we went and everything we did so you can finally believe me."

She looks at him with incredulity and holds his stare awkwardly, as if he'll cave and admit his lies. When he holds her stare without averting his eyes, her eyebrows fall, and her shoulders sag.

She begins to smile sheepishly at him and then speaks so softly that I almost can't hear her. "You've got to admit this would be a good place to hide"—she lifts and opens her arm, gesturing at the clearing—"especially when we have all those people back at the camper."

Her eyebrows lift suggestively, and she winks at him.

"Are you serious? You went from yelling at me, accusing me of cheating, to wanting to have sex?" he asks her, raising his voice.

"Well, now that you've proved you guys were just making wind, I don't see why not," she explains to him.

He shakes his head and says, "How about because I'm not in the mood after all that bullshit?"

She bats her eyelashes and says, "Come on, it'll be fun. It's not like you need to pull out or use a condom since we're already expecting."

As she rubs her belly, her wedding ring catches my attention as it sparkles in the sun.

"By all means, I still have to show you all of our other stops from earlier. The last thing I need is you doing some reverse psychology on me. If I agree to have sex with you right now, I feel like afterward, you'd only use that as proof that I did just that with Yasmin," he says to her, lowering his voice as he goes.

She laughs, an authentic deep laugh at his statement, before saying, "Dang, you know me so well. Okay, fine, let's go and finish our tour."

He shakes his head at her statement and starts the golf cart again. That bitch—Julia is her name—pulls him in for a kiss before they leave.

I watch them go, shaking my head as well. What kind of sadistic nonsense was that? He's married to her? So he did cheat on her with the other woman—Yasmin, apparently— and he lied about it. I don't blame him. Despite my limited knowledge of Julia, I do know that just about every exhale she makes is accompanied by an insult. I wouldn't stay committed to that nonsense either. That's basically why my mom and dad aren't together, if I had to venture a reason.

Of course, in regard to my parent's relationship, my behavior didn't help. All my mom did was complain about me and complain about Dad. She nagged the both of us. For me, it made me want to act out more and do things that would piss her off. Dad must have thought the same thing because he cheated on her.

I always noticed that he was gone a lot because I was happy when he wasn't home. Disappearing for a whole night some-times, always with an excuse ready for Mom and me. I'm surprised she didn't realize it sooner, as often as he'd wander off.

I heard them fighting the night my mom must have found out, so they really never had a chance to lie to me about it. I always heard things that they didn't want me to hear. She even told him once that she prayed I wouldn't turn out to be like him. Which is something I never really understood, as my father and

I are nothing alike.

After she found out that he was having an affair, she forgave him and stayed around. She tried to stop nagging so much, but I don't think she could help it. Ultimately, she couldn't get over him cheating on her, and she constantly threw it in his face, always making crude remarks. Over time, their relationship became too dysfunctional, and they ultimately divorced.

My dad never seemed bothered by it. He seemed happy to not have to provide excuses for his disappearing acts and lucky that I was at an age where he was able to leave me alone at home. I was left in their wreckage and forced to go back and forth between homes. I was left adjusting to a new normal, suffering for their sins. A family ruined. All because my mom couldn't stop complaining about everything. Just like that bitch Julia.

I ball my fists as I think about how hateful my mom can be to me and my dad. Julia reminds me so much of her. At least my mom had a valid reason to complain about me. I'm not perfect. But this chick has nothing to be mad about, and she is still stirring the pot. I hate her even more than I hate my mom.

That's when a thought crosses my mind. I am the only one who gets to decide my future. I won't run, I won't go, and I won't wait it out. They think I'm bad now? They haven't seen what I'm capable of, but they're about to. I'm going to take another route, truly be myself, and remove the restraints on my soul. Let's see what they think about me then.

Chapter Twenty-Four

CJ

Then

When I returned to our tent earlier, Dad was angry. I think he tried to be understanding initially, but I must have spooked him when I stayed away for so long. It makes sense. He thought he lost me. He probably got in his own head, started thinking that I must have found out about his plan, and figured I'd tried to run away. I can't say the thought didn't cross my mind. I've decided I have different plans for me and dear ol' Dad. He only further sealed his fate when he began berating me for my absence.

Since it's only the two of us out here, he used the opportunity to yell at me and slap me across the face. I didn't say anything. I didn't try to defend myself or lash back. Eventually, he got tired of abusing me, and we just carried on, with me making sandwiches for supper. He made a fire, just for the hell of it.

Now here I am, intrusive thoughts raging through my head. I want to hurt him. I want to hurt him so bad that by extension, I hurt Mom. I want to give them a reason to be scared of me, and want to prove to them that I am the monster that they believe me to be.

But part of me wants to rationalize these feelings, almost as if I'm trying to talk myself out of them. For instance, I keep thinking am I that upset, or is it a combination of all the things in my life that are making me feel this way? Will I always feel this way? Will hurting them resolve anything? Am I even still being shipped off, or have they since changed their minds and I'm blowing this all out of proportion? Is it the betrayal that has planted these vicious impulses, or have I always been like this, a monster trying to break free of my cage?

That snobby bitch from earlier coming around sure didn't do anything to brighten my spirits. I keep thinking about how, if she had she not shown up in the clearing, I may have made it back here to avoid my beating. I could have had a great day, had it not been for her incessant bitching, in general.

Overall, I would have had a great weekend had she not been here to ruin almost every day. She even went as far as making rude remarks about us, despite the fact that she knew we could likely hear her.

Engrossed in reliving today's events while I sit by the fire with Dad asleep in the tent, I hardly notice the sound of tires in the distance. I move my head just enough to glance behind me, and the light of the fire creates dancing shadows among the trees.

Even through the dense forestry and the shadows cast by nightfall, I'd recognize that bright-yellow object anywhere. I wonder who's in it this time. They look like they've come to a stop. I begin to watch them from the corner of my eye. They're very quiet this time around, so I start to think that Julia must not be one of them. But I do see two women out of the corner of my eye, and again my curiosity takes over.

I slowly ease out of my seat, trying to make it appear as if I may be going in or behind our tent, but I ease my movements in the opposite direction, ducking into the dark shadows created by the dense trees. Without thinking, I begin to inch toward them. As I get closer, I quickly recognize that monster of a woman as well as one of the other women from their party.

I should walk away. I know I should, but I continue to creep toward them, unsure of what I'll do when I reach them. They're distracted, looking up at the sky through the scattered holes in the trees above.

Everything that happens next is a blur. The indignation inside me grows rapidly, eradicating the control that I thought I had. It's as if I transform from human being to demon, and in that moment, I know what I'm going to do.

I run up to that evil woman and pull her from her seat, throwing her to the ground. A roar erupts from me as I look up at the sky, throwing my hands to my sides, clenching them into fists. When I look back, I see the other woman in the passenger seat, frozen, staring at her friend on the ground. I have no quarrel with her, but she remains there, motionless and blank.

Her friend Julia is watching me similarly from the ground, her head twisted upward. Initially, her fall disoriented her, but I can see her gears spinning, as she places her hands firmly on the ground, attempting to pick herself up.

Luckily for me, she is on her stomach, so I quickly put one foot down on her back to keep her from getting up. My foot on her back doesn't deter her, though, as she continues to struggle. The other woman remains there, staring at her friend. She probably hates her as much as I do and is thankful that I'm interfering. That thought, inspired by the other woman's submission, is all the permission that I need before I continue my assault. I remove my foot from her back to kick her. Julia grunts in pain and rolls onto her back.

I know a normal person who'd lost control of their faculties would stop now, realizing the severity of what they started, harming an innocent woman, but not me. What I'm feeling is quite the opposite. I'm craving to hurt her more, to make her scream and watch blood spurt from the open wounds inflicted by my hand. Especially this woman, who has been nothing but horrible since the moment I saw her. This woman who reminds me so much of my mother, whom I've come to despise.

I bend down and begin to lift her by her shoulders, but she resists me, trying to escape my grasp. I squeeze my hands around her neck instead and hoist her up to meet my glare. As I stare into her eyes, I notice her attempt to avert them, trying to escape my grip and her fate. I feel her throat vibrate under my hands as she attempts to scream for help. As I watch her, I relish in the power I hold over her, the ability to diminish her and silence her, before I gradually release my control. I let her limp body fall to the ground. She's still conscious but, most importantly, afraid. Now she recognizes I am the predator and that she is to be my prey.

I drop to my knees, simultaneously pulling my pocket knife from my pants. I flip open the blade swiftly before she has a chance to get some of her fight back, before her friend can try to stop me.

I plunge the blade into her chest. I savor the sight. My knife cuts through her clothing and skin easily, leaving a piercing wound that begins to gush blood as I remove the blade. That simply will not be enough to kill her, so I lift my arm to deliver more tantalizing torture, eager to bring the knife down again and again. Her scream is frantic, and it cuts through my pleasure. I look down at Julia's eyes, rolling back into her head, and quickly realize the scream is coming from the other woman.

I turn my head to find that she has finally found the courage to make a move. I'm not surprised to see her scrambling from her perch, and I decide right then that I'm going to let her go. She isn't important, as I have much more I'd like to do to Julia.

I hear shuffling from our tent, and I look up to see my dad's head peeking out, trying to determine the source of the sound. Ideally, she'll run away quietly, leaving me here to torture her friend, and he'll go back to bed, unaware of what's unfolding in the woods.

That thought quickly disappears as my dad locks eyes with the woman trying to escape, and she starts screaming, "Help me, please! *Help! Help!*"

Chapter Twenty-Five

CJ

Then

So, here we are. Me and Dad. Burying bodies together. Cannot say I thought anything like this would ever happen. He buries Julia as I bury this other woman, piling lump upon lump of moist earth atop her lifeless body. Stupid, stupid woman. She almost got away.

I was so involved in the moment that I didn't care if she got away. She made a crucial mistake, though. She thought that my dad would help her. And honestly, I thought he would too. So imagine my surprise when he smashed a rock down over her head a couple times, taking her out for good.

Now we both stand here, secreting buckets of sweat. The breeze of the night isn't nearly strong enough to keep us cool as we labor over their graves.

I've never related to my dad as much as I did the moment he struck the woman over the head. But even now, I don't know why he did it. I think it might be to protect himself and his image. I may as well start to come up with my defense now. I mean, one of us needs to talk about this at some point.

"She was so mean, so hateful, and such a bitch. Just like Mom. Don't you get it. Don't you see why I did what I did?" I reason with him.

He doesn't say anything, though. So I continue. I've got to make him understand. He didn't see everything that I saw, but he's got to be disgusted with me. There's no way I can redeem myself, but I have to try.

"Probably not. You only see me for all my faults."

"You've got to realize something," he tells me before stopping, motioning for me to continue my efforts.

"What?" I ask him pleadingly before I continue shoveling the dirt atop the body, although it's rained so much that it's more like mud. The recently upturned ground fills the surrounding air with a distinctly earthy smell.

"I'm now realizing how similar you are to me," he says. "Now, I never did anything like this. Not as young as you are, at least. No offense, but I was more methodical and old enough to cover my tracks.

"You are my son, and I'm not upset with you. I know what you are going through. I have felt the way that you feel. I hoped that your behavior was normal teenage brooding. I should have been more understanding, but I was hoping you'd be more like your mother and this was a phase. I don't want you to have to live the way that I do, but now that I know what you are capable of, I have to accept it. And if you'll let me, I can help you."

I'm shocked, my mouth hanging slightly agape, as he points down at our handiwork.

"This will be your first lesson. I'll help you hide these bodies, and we will erase every trace that we were here. They might find their remains, but they'll never find us. I'll show you how to manipulate those around you so that you won't get caught for this. You won't get caught for anything that you do. I do understand you. Even more than you realize."

III

Part Three

Chapter Twenty-Six

Brooke

Then

You always hear that your life flashes before your eyes when you die. You read about it in books and see it on shows, and I think they even made a movie or docuseries about it. Now, as visions come and go, I surmise that they must be talking about this experience, the one I'm having now.

I see myself as a child climbing a tree. At the library, checking out a book. At a sleepover with friends. In class, focused on the teacher. Teaching my little brother how to ride a bike. Watching TV with my husband. Running errands for the day.

None of these images are of monumental elements of my life. Actually, they're all snippets of life that one might easily forget. But now, as death is imminent and I struggle to breathe, I understand them all for what they were. Precious moments that made me the person that I am. If I could do something to save myself, I would. I want to have more moments like this. I want to continue to live life and appreciate all the small things, leisurely waiting for the big moments to happen and enjoying them all the same.

Why can't I make more of these visions, these steps in life? All I have to do is fight. I have to try. I can't expect to change anything if I just lie here and die. I have a reason to try, and so I will.

The first thing I do is feel around in an attempt to find the edge of the sheet that encases my body. If it weren't for this sheet, I would have inhaled the dirt and likely suffocated by now. I begin to shake. I was unconscious and able to conserve some oxygen that was trapped underneath the sheet with me, it seems, but now my breathing has become more erratic, indicated by the heat I feel wash over my face with every exasperated breath. I need to remove my safety net so that I can dig myself free without obstruction. I take a deep breath as I outline the steps I need to follow in order to free myself before I run out of air.

I take a deep breath and squeeze my eyes firmly shut, pulling the sheet to my side, struggling under the weight of the ground that rests atop me. I keep my lips pursed and refuse to breathe through my nose, afraid that instead of oxygen I'll breathe in dust and debris, thwarting my escape.

I begin to wiggle my shoulders, loosening the dirt that surrounds me. Next, I move my midsection, my hips, and then my legs, continuously loosening the dirt surrounding the bedsheet I find myself entrapped in.

Once I make some room around my body, I start to comb the dirt that's encompassing my hand. It's so thick that I can grab large chunks all at once. Just as I'm about to reach up, a thought hits me. I hope that I'm buried on my back. I think that I'm digging upward, but I could actually be digging downward.

I quickly think back to how I heard the men speaking earlier, and from the direction their voices were coming from, I'm positive that I should go up. God, I hope I'm right. I have to move fast. There's no time to overthink it and absolutely no time for me to be wrong. I also don't think that I have the luxury of time to pray for my survival.

I'm lucky that I'm not dead yet. *Not dead yet.* Those words resonate with me, and I ferociously begin to worm myself free. There's got to be a way out of here. I have to try, and so I continue on.

I dig and dig, and I put all my strength into my efforts because I know I won't be able to move like this for much longer. I'm still alive. As the thought winds through me, my fingers burst forward to find nothing. Nothing, as in no dirt, which means fresh air! Oh my god, I'm almost out. I lunge my entire body up through the dirt and some smaller, heavier areas that must be mud and wind up sitting in my grave, half buried. Something that I never imagined I'd be capable of, something I never imagined I'd have to live through.

Before attempting to open my eyes, I wipe the dry dirt and smaller clumps of moist mud from my face and hesitantly open my eyelids. I have emerged through the hole that I created to see what appears to still be the dead of night with little to no light visible through the trees. I'm hungry for air, inhaling bits of dirt with each greedy breath, which coincidentally causes me to cough repeatedly. I spit more dirt out before I take another breath, an attempt to center myself. I exhale slowly and look around. The ground around me is splotchy, both dry and wet. The trees appear to have shielded certain areas from the rain, leaving dry patches on the ground.

It's calm. Quiet, too, and I don't see anyone as I turn my head side to side. I cast my eyes downward to gauge the extent to which my lower body is submerged in the moist earth. How disgraceful that this grave is so shallow but also how blessed. Any deeper and my efforts would have been in vain. I would think they'd have made sure I was dead before burying me.

It seems that they must have been rushed because that appears not to be the case. They're gone, and all that remains to the eye is another mound of dirt five feet away. I don't think this is where we were when that monster attacked Julia, although I can't be sure. It looks different here—or I think so, at least. I take one more glance around to ensure I'm safe and alone before I let the tears wash down my filthy cheeks. Julia's gone. The baby... I couldn't save her, save *them*, and honestly, I didn't even try. I shake the thoughts from my head. My fight's not over yet. I dig my hands into the surrounding land to hoist myself up. I still have to get back to my family.

Chapter Twenty-Seven

Brooke

Then

I don't have to walk long before I hear the approach of vehicles. Jacob's truck appears over a crested hill, and I fall to my knees in relief. Jacob and Kent scurry out of the truck, rushing to my side.

"Brooke! God, you're bleeding," Kent says as he wraps his arms around me. Jacob stands there, looking around me for Julia, I presume.

I lock eyes with him when he doesn't find her.

"Where's Julia?" he asks me, his voice shaking.

My head drops, and tears begin to fall down my cheeks, likely leaving defining trails through the muck on my face as they crash onto the rain-slicked grass below. I don't know how to answer. He can't save her. She's already dead. I cry harder at the thought, struggling to breathe, sobbing and gasping for air.

"Brooke." His voice hardens. "Where is my wife?"

"I-I-I-I didn't mean it. I'm sorry."

Shit. Why'd I have to say it like that? This is no way for him to find out his wife's dead. There's no good way, but this has to be one of the worst.

"What did you do?" he demands, awaiting my answer.

"I'll show you," I mumble to him through a break in my sobs as I push myself off the ground and away from the safety of Kent's arms.

As we walk the short way back, sirens begin to echo through the trees. Just as we reach the place where Julia is buried, I watch as police cars pull up, their tires flinging dust that visibly falls slowly back to earth through the emergency lights and headlights of the police cars.

Upon seeing the mound of dirt, highlighted by the beams of light coming from the surrounding vehicles, Jacob doesn't hesitate. Running toward it quickly, he soon drops to his knees and begins to dig, as does Kent.

Their efforts are futile, and that thought alone breaks me down further. I begin to drift from my body. This is too much too fast. I'm too weak for this. I begin to dissociate as I fall to the ground.

* * *

Everything that happens after that is a blur of voices, visions, memories, movement, and emotions.

I'm lifted from the ground—by who, I don't know. New and unfamiliar faces appear in front of me, voices muffled. They appear to be talking to me, their eyes looking into mine, but it's as if my brain's ability to process information has given out. Nothing is coming through.

One moment I'm at the campground, and the next, I'm sitting in an ambulance.

Blink.

I'm in a car.

Blink.

I'm in an interrogation room.

Blink.

Same room, but a man sits across from me. His lips move, but all I hear is static.

Blink.

He's gone.

Blink.

He's back.

"Brooke."

I acknowledge my name by lifting my chin, trying to focus on the first word that's broken through to my distorted reality.

My guilt is the one thing I'm able to sense clearly, even more distinct than the rhythm of my still–beating heart.

"I know you've been through a lot. But we need to catch whoever did this," he says to me.

I stare at him. my thoughts racing.

I'm guilty. I could have tried to save her. We could have either both survived or both died, but I was too selfish to risk my life to save hers. In retrospect, it's not fair that I get to be here and she doesn't.

"I'm the reason she's dead," I mutter.

* * *

"Where'd you get the knife?" the man asks me.

I liked it a lot better when I couldn't hear them, when I had the luxury of impaired comprehension.

I stopped answering hours ago, or maybe it's been days, but the officers haven't given up on me. Their demeanor has remained stoic. I'm not sure if they wish to condemn me or absolve me with their line of questioning.

"Your husband says he doesn't recognize it. He says he doesn't recognize you. He's told us that you would never hurt anyone."

Ah, Kent. So admirable to try to defend me. My husband's right. I wouldn't hurt anyone, not intentionally. Or so I thought. But I didn't defend Julia, so in essence, doesn't that make the harm that was caused, the life that was taken, intentional?

"Who killed Julia? Don't you want the murderer brought to justice?"

Again, I don't respond. I stare down into my lap as the barrage continues.

"If you killed her, why were you also covered in dirt?"

"Why go through such lengths to frame yourself as innocent, only to admit guilt?"

"Are you aware that Mrs. Julia's husband was having an affair with Mrs. Yasmin?"

Now, that shocks me, but I will not acknowledge his question with a response. I'm surprised that Julia's cheating accusation held some merit. I wonder if she knew more than she let on.

"Did you conspire with her husband? Were you two also romantically involved?"

How dare he. I close my eyes. He's baiting me. Or he really thinks so little of me. I did betray my friend but not in the way that he's implying.

"You tried to cover your deceit, and we would have believed you innocent given some of the evidence. But you failed when your husband and Mr. Jacob found you. You couldn't lie to them as easily as you intended to."

Interesting. He says it as if it is a statement, not a question. Does he believe that, or is he trying to provoke me to speak?

"We received an anonymous call. The caller witnessed a serious verbal altercation between a female individual and the deceased. The description they provided ID's you as the one they saw arguing with Julia shortly before she was found murdered."

I cringe at the reminder of her death and the false accusation made against me.

Won't they just leave me alone to rot inside myself?

"You do realize that even if you don't tell us what happened, we still have enough evidence and probable cause to convict you of murder and sentence you to prison?" the man says bluntly.

Good. Let them.

The way I see it, an act of betrayal is an act of betrayal regardless of how the police and media decide to spin it.

I may not be guilty of murder, but I'm basically an accessory to it, and I deserve to be punished.

Sorry, Kent. Sorry, Erin. I should have died that night too.

Chapter Twenty-Eight

Brooke

Now

That smile. It's the first time my new psychiatrist has smiled since we met here at the day program. He looks so familiar, but all I've seen in my prison are the other patients and staff, and I haven't seen anyone from the outside in years. I know he isn't a therapist that I've had before because I would remember wouldn't I?

We sit here, in a dance of wills. He is as relentless in his attempts at conversation as I am at responding to them. So we sit and mostly stare at one another. His thoughts are unknown to me, as mine remain unknown to him.

Just like the heat lighting from that night that crashed through the darkness, his smile now breaks through the fog. My jaw slackens at the realization. That's why I don't feel comfortable talking to him. It dawns on me like a wave crashing onto the shore. He was there that night. He knows the truth. He knows who killed Julia.

I freeze. I need to think. Will he try to hurt me? Is h

attempting to silence me now, as if I haven't already been silenced enough?

I can't help but wonder, will anyone else ever know the truth? Will he allow it? So I'll ask him. What do I have to lose?

"Will anyone ever know what happened that night?" I ask, trying not to reveal too much to him about my sudden recollection.

He doesn't ignore my inquiry, nor does he acknowledge it. He pauses, seeming to ponder how he'll proceed. Does he realize that I recognize him?

"I'd like to help you remember that night. In due time, of course."

That deep voice resonates. I tried so hard all this time to forget that night, and I was successful. Apparently I was so good at blocking it all out that I forgot important details. Details I can now share with the police to help them find Julia's murderer. I can't believe I didn't recognize his voice sooner.

"I don't need your help," I snap at him, unable to keep the frustration at bay any longer. "You were there. You tried to kill me. You're not going to help me. You want to make sure I stay here to rot!"

"Brooke, please, calm down. Truly, you can't believe that?" he asks me, the hint of a smirk on his lips.

That smug son of a bitch. He has some balls. It wasn't enough to let me take the blame for Julia's murder, but now he strides in here after all this time, just to mess with me?

Think, Brooke, think.

Maybe I can get him to say something that will prove he was there that night, prove he helped the true murderer evade capture. Prove that he tried to kill me and buried me alive. If he risked being identified just to taunt me, he'll probably get off on bragging about how easy it was to evade capture.

"I'm stunned. I wondered how that kid was so smart, how he was able to hide any evidence that he was there," I explain to him, feigning admiration. "But now it all makes sense. He had your help. He couldn't have done it so successfully without you. Impressive, especially since my survival wasn't part of the plan, I'm sure."

He stares at me, deciding what to do next. Deciding how to respond to my provocation.

After a moment, he looks around the room and then emits an almost-demonic chuckle before narrowing his eyes on me.

"Well, if you're eager to tell us what happened the night your friend was murdered, we can start right away," he says, almost as if still feigning ignorance. Toying with my emotions, as if it's his favorite game.

I'll craft a story, sprinkle some untruths in, and see if he'll call my bluff, eager to finally reveal himself.

"That boy murdered my friend. He hit her over the head before stabbing her to death. I froze, and he used that moment to chase me. He thought he'd be able to kill me before you showed up. He hit me so hard with that rock. It's a miracle that the first blow didn't kill me. You tried to save me. Why didn't you save me?" I plead with him. True tears form in the corners of my eyes as I recall what actually happened. How he was the one who tried to kill me with that damn rock. My tears are authentic, not forced. Not an act in an attempt to appeal to his emotional side. I doubt I'd have any luck in that department.

He watches me, his face void of emotion. When he speaks again, I wonder how I didn't recognize his voice sooner.

"Tsk, tsk, tsk, Brooke. How are we to ever make progress toward your mental wellness if you can't be honest with me?"

He manages to deter me without acknowledging my accusations. He's a slippery serpent, slithering gracefully against my inquisition, reluctant to admit to any form of responsibility.

I may as well prod him and get answers to some of the questions I've always had. Maybe I can use what I get from him against him. Allow myself a chance to obtain my freedom after all this time. I may have been silent once, but I won't be silent forever.

"You drove the golf cart to the archery lanes. Why? We were missing, and they were bound to launch a search party on the grounds to find us."

My confidence and my question get him on the hook. I can tell as his devious smile begins to widen that he wants to gloat. He thrives off ensuring my defeat. Identifying my new resolve sparks a hunger in him. The need to break me down again is insatiable, and he is unable to resist an opportunity to defeat me once more.

"I knew that. I also knew that the last thing I wanted them to find is where she was actually killed, leading them closer to finding evidence against my son," he rationalizes quietly.

"I wanted them to think a stranger murdered you both. I wanted to ensure that they never suspected another camper but rather a lone traveler passing through. I actually chose that area for the irony. Burying my son's target, near targets," he explains to me with a chuckle.

"Luckily for you, me being alive didn't get them any closer to finding you guys," I say, casting my eyes to the floor. "It actually gave them a target to focus on."

"Oh yes. I wish I could take credit and say it was all intentional, but alas, it is by sheer luck that they focused on pursuing you as the murderer." He pauses before continuing. "Well, that anonymous tip that I called in informing them that I saw you and her arguing in that area helped, of course."

My eyes widen in surprise.

"Well, can you blame me?" he asks. "I couldn't have them considering there was another killer. I had to ensure that they believed it was you. I had to guarantee that they would never suspect anyone else and that we would never be seen as suspects.

"I knew it would be hard for the police to find and identify us, but nothing is ever certain. Regardless, we tried to eliminate any signs of us being there. We made sure that we left no prints behind, and the rain helped tremendously. Oh, and I work here, of course," he says, opening his arms in demonstration. "The staff has access to the campgrounds through this facility without having to check in at the front gate. My son and I decided to stay here on a whim. So as it happens, there was no record of us even being here officially."

Unbelievable. This is Camp Sunshine, the same one we saw in the campground? I could vomit, being so close to the scene of the murder and not even realizing it. It's preposterous that I'm here, at the beginning of my end.

"Why me? I had a family," I ask.

"Then you can understand my dilemma. I did it for my family. To protect my son," he growls.

He won't get away with this. I won't let him.

I lunge at him before he sees it coming. I have no weapons, but the anger that's been growing inside me since he began speaking erupts. I bite him viciously, grinding my teeth into his flesh, intending to make his arm gush blood. Without looking, I claw at his face as he yells for help.

I release the grip of my jaw on his arm in order to focus long enough to dig my thumbs into his eyeballs when I'm suddenly pulled away, and my vision begins to fade. This bastard. Of course the orderlies think they need to protect him, even though they should actually be protecting me.

I know what happened that night now. I've always known. It's just been so foggy, and the truth, so elusive.

Julia wasn't a great person, and of course no one deserves to die like that, but it happened nonetheless. With all the time that has passed, I've convinced myself that everything was the way it was for a reason. It was fair for me to suffer for not trying harder to save her. I deserved this punishment for not trying to help a woman and her unborn child, resting unaware and defenseless in her mother's womb. I was at peace, or as close as I could get to peace, knowing that she had to die, whether I had a hand in it or not. Regardless of who wielded the blade that took her life, I'm still guilty.

My eyelids fall, my muscles loosen, and my thoughts weaken, as does my resolve. We're both accessories to Julia's murder, but he's a doctor, and I'm a psychiatric patient. They'll never believe me.

Chapter Twenty-Nine

Brooke

Now

They drugged me. They have drugged me, continue to drug me, and will drug me again. I lie in my bed now, having woken up to that demonic presence at my bedside. I'm unsure how long he lingered, but I know it was long enough to watch me fade in and out of consciousness. Long enough to show me that he wasn't going anywhere, that he wasn't afraid of me. Just as I was afraid of his son, I now have that same terror toward his father.

Initially, when I was convicted of Julia's murder, I didn't defend myself. The way I saw it, I had two options. When I thought about my first option, it played out like this—if I was fortunate, they'd believe my innocence, pursue another lead and free me to go home to my family. But I couldn't live with what I'd done, or instead, what I didn't do. I could have done things differently. Intervened, attempted to stop him, or even just distracted him long enough so that Julia had a fighting chance. I could have helped so she wouldn't have been caught completely off guard and enabled her to be better equipped to defend herself. But I was scared. Scared that I'd get hurt. So scared that I let her suffer. She was scared too. The entire time that he hurt her, she was probably rationalizing in her head that I would save her, that I would help her. I didn't. For that, I'm guilty. In good conscience, I couldn't go home. Home to my family, living right next door to the family that I destroyed. Julia couldn't make it back to her family. Therefore, it would be unfair for me to return to mine.

Those thoughts led me to the second option, the one that I chose. I willingly allowed them to cast blame on me. I wasn't purely innocent. So I took the blame and sulked in misery all these years.

While imprisoned, I continued imagining what my life would have been like had I tried to defend myself. I'd envision my intact family outside, spending time together, while doom and dismay lived next door. Every day, I would see a family that I helped destroy. I'm sure Jacob and Rachel relocated as far away from my family as they could once I received my conviction. Hell, I don't even know if Kent and Erin still occupy our home.

I willingly took my punishment. Now that I've obtained additional information, it doesn't change anything. Even if I were to go home now, after all this time... I'll never get back what I lost. Time doesn't rewind. God, how I wish I could turn back time.

I can't go back, but I can go forward.

Suddenly, hope flows through me, a white light defeating the darkness. I've accepted my punishment, but I shouldn't have to continue to live like this. I didn't murder Julia, and now that I know who did, I can move on. This way, I receive my punishment, but so do they.

I've missed many of Erin's milestones. I've missed watching her grow into a young girl. So I go home, and what? Everything goes back to normal? Probably not. Not anytime soon, at least. She doesn't know me. She likely doesn't even remember me. I've already missed so much of her life. I used to see it as if she were better off without me around.

This new light shines, showing me possibilities I never dared imagine.

I could be there when she graduates high school.

I could be there when she gets married.

I can watch her become a mom.

I can explain my inaction, and with time, she can forgive me,

Despite the drugs weakening my senses, I feel a surge of pressure. A wave of resilience pulses through the room, almost tangible.

I know Kent well, and I know he'll never look at me the same. I know that although our love appeared eternal, it has faded. Marred by my choices. Our relationship is like that dilapidated gazebo, left to crumble and fade into nonexistence. Disheveled and unable to be repaired after such a long time without care, without maintenance. Kent and Erin don't even visit me here.

He may never forgive me, as ours was a love forged in the fires of youth. But Erin... our love was forged at her birth. A bond meant to hold despite all that can try to break it.

No longer will I resign myself to staying here, held prisoner, while the rest of the world goes on without me in it. No longer will I wait for my body to crumble, alongside my mind, into an unsalvageable wreck, awaiting demolition.

No more.

Instead, I'll tear away all the ugly ruined bits, and I'll start over again at the studs. I'll build myself back up into the woman

I used to be.

Chapter Thirty

Brooke

Now

Once the drugs finally wear off, the orderlies explain to me that I almost lost my day-program rights but that my therapist is willing to forgive my actions.

I listen to what they tell me and take it in slowly, but after they leave my room, my thoughts begin to flurry with countless ideas. I try to center my thoughts, but it's difficult after years of cocooning myself, hiding. I would block out memories, possibilities, ideas, and interpretations, choosing instead to remain in the solitude of the empty nest I created out of misery.

I take in a ragged breath in an attempt to concentrate.

Good, Dr. G still wishes to toy with me. That's the only reason I can see that he'd defend my actions to others.

I can use that to my advantage. He's smart, but I have to be smarter.

Given what little I know about him, I wager he thinks that his interactions with me will be a game. He knows who I am. He was unsure if I'd recognize him, but he enjoyed the fact that I did. He is my therapist, so ultimately he has to adhere to a code of ethics. Ha. But in order to keep up the facade, he will have to, or at least make it seem to others, act as if he is helping me.

I've seen patients from here recover before. With time and dedication, they can heal, and then they can leave. I'm not sure if they go home, another facility, or to prison, but I know that healing can be accomplished.

I'll lead him to believe he is helping me. It's foreign to me... healing. But I can do it. I'll do it without him. I'll heal in spite of him.

One thing that I don't understand is his endgame. What does he think treating me as one of his patients is going to accomplish?

It can't be that he actually wants me to grow, because doesn't that mean I'd want to seek justice for Julia? Doesn't he realize that, ideally, I'd have him and his son convicted? Surely, he'll use these sessions to try to break me down further.

Unless, in his twisted mind, he thinks he can actually help me recover from my trauma. Maybe he gets off on the sense that he destroyed me but is also able to rebuild me. Some type of god complex.

Or he thinks he can manipulate me. That seems more likely. He can't be so stupid as to actually help me, leading me to seek absolution. Maybe he wants to play with my medication, toy with my mind, and drive me into an indefinite silence.

No matter his intent, my goal will remain the same. I will bide my time. Identify his plan. Obtain any incriminating evidence that I can in an unassuming manner. And lastly, I'll destroy him and his son. Just like they destroyed me. Just like they destroyed Julia. I may not have saved her in that moment, but no matter how long it takes, I'll spend the rest of my life trying to make amends in the shadows so that I may once again thrive in the light.

Chapter Thirty-One

Dr. G

Now

I was there that night, and I hold the power. Actually, I always have. I decide how this ends, and shit, I even decided how this started. Poor Brooke never even had a chance. She never knew what she was going up against.

I have always been methodical, which ultimately led me to this career path. I've always been very studious and fascinated by the mind and its diseases, as well as how it can be manipulated.

Even my own son, Clayton Gemeinhardt Jr., fell for my tactics. All I had to do was push him to the edges of his anger and stoke the already-burning embers of his inheritance—my genetics. I've studied him his whole life, as if he were the sole subject in my own experiment, and I know everything that makes him tick. That night, I deceived him, telling him that I didn't know he was an evil soul, but how could I not know? He's my son, my blood, my experiment.

No, I've always been there, molding him, grooming him,

fostering his potential.

However, working with Brooke is challenging. I didn't know as much about her as I do my son. So I learned more about her. I studied her breakdown after the incident. I can't deny that I was scared, terrified our downfall would be brought about by her survival. I was vigilant, and I followed the TV and news reports for days. All it took was one journalist's report, documenting her appearance upon being found and her inability to speak about her friend's murder, to streamline my scheme to make her the scapegoat.

I called in that anonymous tip, and she's been the primary suspect since then. To the best of my knowledge, the police never conducted a thorough investigation on any additional suspects, and even if they had, it would have been difficult to identify my son and me. Her ability to survive terrified me at first, but it was ultimately the key to us escaping prosecution.

Since Julia's death, I've trained my son in my ways, and he now performs many of the sinful acts I once used to enjoy. I decided to pull back the reins a little. Let him have his fun. If we were both out there killing, it might lead others to discover us, and I can't have that happen after all that I've done to shield us from being discovered by the authorities.

I waited a very cautious period of time before seeing Brooke. It helped that she was too unstable to be assigned to my primary facility. Meanwhile, I continued to read reports, research the case, and investigate inconspicuously in an attempt to ensure there was nothing to suggest another suspect. Specifically, nothing to identify my son and me.

I didn't want to involve myself in her care early on, as I didn't want her to recognize me and change her story. So I stalked her in the background, putting time between us. I truly thought after all this time that she wouldn't recognize me and I could actually help her return to a sense of normalcy. I loved the irony that I helped destroy her and that I'd also help avenge her. By now, so much time has passed, the odds that the police would discover any evidence to prosecute my son and me are nil.

Alas, she did recognize me. An exciting update. One that made me cautious to proceed.

Initially, after I confessed to her, she hid in the recesses of her mind, becoming fully mute. That day she attacked me, I wove a stupendous story for the others—she was in a fragile state, and this was too much for her too soon; I was fine, but we should really be focused on accommodating her so she could be fine too.

I even sat in her room afterward. I waited for the drugs to wear off to ensure that she knew I wasn't going anywhere. I stood there, looming, showing her who was in control of the situation.

There was no more fight left in her upon this revelation. My reintroduction put the nail in the coffin of her demise. Funny how I say that since we buried her in the ground without a coffin.

That was, until they changed some of her medications. She began to talk and was even permitted to return to the day program. We have since resumed treatment sessions with one another.

I've enjoyed our sessions, although they're more akin to games between cat and mouse. The thrill of our interactions is almost as fulfilling as when I cause physical harm to others.

Instead of slicing away, through skin to bone to satisfy my urges, I now supply her with a false sense of security. Knowing that her ability to achieve acceptance and absolution can only be possible by my hands is euphoric. The hands that helped take those things away from her are the only ones that can restore them.

So we sit in my office day after day, recounting the events of her past trauma. I help her navigate her emotions. My interactions with Brooke are truly the best sessions I've ever had, and I live for them. In a way, my involvement allows me to understand her more than anyone else ever could.

I've ensured that my son and I are safe until this point, but I also understand that, in helping her, I risk my freedom and that of my son. I know her so well, though, and I can tell she only wishes now to come to peace with her actions and accept what happened the night my son killed her friend, the first of many of his victims.

I hoped she wouldn't recognize me that day, the day she walked into my office at Camp Sunshine. I was looking forward to manipulating her, working with her, and facilitating her rehabilitation. She, the puppet. And me, the master. I wanted to try to allow her to redeem herself. I owed her that much. I wasn't even sure after all this time that she'd want to be saved. Despite her negative reaction upon identifying me, we have made progress, and I am now able to do what I set out to do with her.

I am thankful for her and her friend because they allowed me and my son to connect on a deeper level, a level I always envisioned for us but one that seemed impossible for the longest time. Who knows if I would have been able to identify and establish that malicious desire in him had they not shown up that weekend?

My son killed that poor girl, Julia, and in my haste to congratulate him and teach him my ways, I didn't ensure that Brooke was dead. That's the conclusion Brooke must have come to also as I stood at her bedside following her attack. A conclusion that she has not even tried to voice despite her newfound love for communication. She has accepted deep down in her core that I am the master and that only I am capable of pulling the strings. She hasn't told anyone about me and my son, and I don't suspect she ever will.

Everything seems to have finally worked out, but rest assured, that's the last time I make a mistake like that. It's been an adventure, but next time, everyone dies, and I'll make sure of it.

A knock sounds on my office door. I wasn't expecting Brooke for her appointment yet, but it's fine. Our sessions are my favorite part of my day.

I flinch as I open the door, as Brooke isn't the one waiting for me on the other side. An officer smiles at me, and I try to hide my shock at his presence.

"Clayton Gemeinhardt?" he asks me.

"Yes, what's this about?"

"You're under arrest," he says, grabbing my arm and flinging me around to place handcuffs around my wrists before continu-ing, "for accessory to murder..." His voice fades as he continues to list additional charges that I am surely guilty enough to receive.

I laugh, a deep, bellowing, demonic chuckle.

Well, well, well. Looks like our sessions have done Brooke some good. Good enough for her to beat me at our little game.

Epilogue

Brooke

Now

A light wind rustles her curly straw-colored hair, which is long enough that it drops well below her petite shoulders. I watch her with adoration, melting into her vivid dark-blue eyes.

Committing the small beauty mark near her left eye to memory.

She's taller than I expected and insists on wearing her hair down, even though she constantly has to remove it from her face.

A light chuckle distracts me, and I turn to Kent.

"She used to say 'It's winding' when the wind would blow her hair all around," he explains to me as he smiles at Erin, now five years old and exploring the playground near our home.

Well, their home.

It would have been too abrupt and unorthodox, given the time I've been gone, for me to just move into her home, our old home, after I was released. I decided to stay with my mother as I try to rebuild the relationship with my husband and daughter. We never divorced, but after all the trauma, you don't just fall back into the normal rhythm of things.

So I visit with them, usually in a neutral public space. Learning about my daughter, her quirks, her personality, and the things she used to say as well as the things she still comes up with.

I'm blessed she's still so young. I have missed so many important parts of her life, but God willing, I'll be around to see more than I have missed.

Kent sits near me, far enough away that we look more like friends than a married couple. We watch our daughter play, and he loves the chance to talk about all the little things that make her so special. I find such solace in that. He could be spiteful and shun me, but he doesn't. He treats me with grace, as if I'm fragile.

I am fragile. I think I've always been. I've become resilient over time. I've had to harden, to strengthen myself so I could stop bending, stop breaking down.

Erin runs up to us, those blue eyes softening in the glare of the sun and in the presence of her father.

"Daddy, can I have a fish?" she asks as she pulls on his pant leg.

I look at him with confusion, but I don't say anything.

He laughs as he begins to rifle through the bag resting near him on the bench before pulling out a bag of gummy candies.

After he opens the bag and hands it to her, he explains to me, "The first time I let her have gummy candy, it was those red fish ones, but now she just calls them all fish. It's too cute, so I've never corrected her."

I smile, a wide grin taking up almost my whole face. It's a smile I never thought I'd have again. Although it pains me to have missed those precious moments, I'm looking forward to being present for all the special ones that are yet to come.

Acknowledgments

Know as I write this, that every single person who discussed this publication with me, your face is flashing through my mind. Thanks to Jillian for brainstorming ideas with me. I couldn't have created this story without your input and contributions. Thanks for inspiring me to bring this story to life. It's pure fiction, with some concepts of real life sprinkled in. Many thanks to my friends and family for encouraging me to complete my manuscript.

Specifically, thanks to my mom for instilling love, kindness, and independence in me throughout my life. Thanks to my dad for pushing me to be the best person that I can be. Thanks to Misty for encouraging my love for books. Thank you to my husband-my best friend, for believing in me and aiding me in this journey. Thank you to my daughter, who has shown me love without limits and has blessed me with the title of "mom." Thanks to my first speed reader, my mother-in-law, I'm the luckiest daughter-in-law and I'll always cherish our relationship. Thanks to Jasmine, who has helped me throughout this entire process and has provided valuable reader feedback that has been incorporated into this book. Most of all, thanks to my grandmother for being my first official reader. I loved sharing and receiving feedback from my initial beta readers/editors: Mawmaw Evelena, Nicole (Gigi), Aunt Celeste (Nana), and Misty (Mimi).

Even if I haven't mentioned your name, because there are so many individuals who have helped provide feedback and guidance during this process, know that I appreciate you! I am so lucky to have you all, and I appreciate the words of encouragement and genuine excitement that you've all shown me through this entire process. I'll never forget the brainstorming sessions, suggestions, excitement, encouragement, and support that everyone in my life has offered.

I'd like to thank Red Adept Editing for providing valuable feedback and insight on this novel. They've opened my eyes to many previously unnoticed aspects of my writing. For instance: I use the word "just" way too much (removed some from the manuscript), I tend to write words in British English (I guess from what I've learned as a voracious reader, also fixed), and I write depressing books (which I have since changed as a result of *that* feedback, in conjunction with the same opinion provided by my beta readers). Doesn't that make you all wonder what the original ending was?

I'd like to thank Get Covers for the cover, and also all the time that they dedicated to making it perfect. Thanks to Kerri for taking the time and creating my ideal cover, but boo on me, as I didn't want to bother her with all the logistics. I'd rather her focus all her time on my handsome Godchild, Zeke. I'd also like to use this time to acknowledge Allison, my other Godchild. Being on the cover of a magazine didn't impress her, but maybe this mention in the back of her Nanny's novel will please her.

Countless coffees, sacrifices, and research have gone into the development and creation of this book and I cannot explain how proud I am! My younger self would be so thrilled to know that I've achieved my lifelong goal of writing a book!

About the Author

Heather Chauvin has always enjoyed writing and story-telling, and loves the challenge of predicting plot twists in both books and movies. She is a Speech-Language Pathologist by day, working with individuals age 0-100 years old. She is passionate about facilitating communication for both children and adults in southern Louisiana. She enjoys reading, board games, and spending time with her husband and young daughter, among other things. Of all her accomplishments, her ability to lick her elbow reigns supreme. Heather often enjoys spiraling into hypothetical situations in her head, as well as with friends, which is the root inspiration for her debut novel, Camp Sunshine. Find her on Facebook!

9 798991 140911